Everything But a Wedding

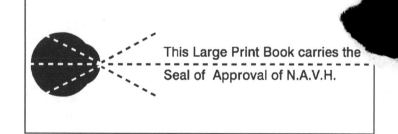

EVERYTHING BUT A WEDDING

HOLLY JACOBS

THORNDIKE PRESS
A part of Gale, Cengage Learning

Detroit • New York • San Francisco • New Haven, Conn • Waterville, Maine • London

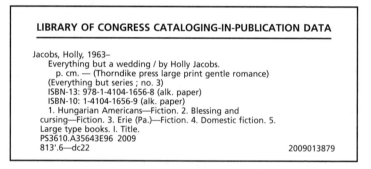

LIBRARY OF CONGRESS CATALOGING-IN-PUBLICATION DATA

Jacobs, Holly, 1963–
    Everything but a wedding / by Holly Jacobs.
      p. cm. — (Thorndike press large print gentle romance)
    (Everything but series ; no. 3)
    ISBN-13: 978-1-4104-1656-8 (alk. paper)
    ISBN-10: 1-4104-1656-9 (alk. paper)
    1. Hungarian Americans—Fiction. 2. Blessing and
cursing—Fiction. 3. Erie (Pa.)—Fiction. 4. Domestic fiction. 5.
Large type books. I. Title.
PS3610.A35643E96 2009
813'.6—dc22
                        2009013879

Published in 2009 by arrangement with Thomas Bouregy & Co., Inc.

Printed in the United States of America
1 2 3 4 5 6 7 13 12 11 10 09

My *Everything But . . .* series
is about family.
This book is for all my
nieces and nephews:
Shane, Brandon, Hannah,
Kristen, J.R., Nick,
Patrick, Hanni, Liesl,
Brigitta, Amelia, Madison,
Sarah, and last,
but by no means least, Regan.

PROLOGUE:

THE SALO FAMILY WEDDING CURSE

Nana Vancy, the matriarch of the Salo family, was depressed.

The whole family knew it.

Dori Salo knew it better than the rest.

Nana had been depressed ever since Dori's brother, Noah, married Callie Smith. It wasn't that Nana didn't love Callie — Dori knew she did. It was that Nana Vancy had hoped they'd be the ones to break the Salo Family Wedding Curse.

The curse her grandmother felt she'd brought down upon the family.

The curse her grandmother so desperately wanted to help break.

Dori Salo felt her grandmother's curse more keenly than the rest of the family because she knew her grandmother was now counting on *her* to break the *imaginary* Salo Family Wedding Curse.

To be fair, although the entire family thought the curse was just in Nana's head, their grandmother believed in it heart and soul. And Dori loved her enough to do anything, promise anything, if she'd only cheer up.

"Nana, you have to come out!" Dori called through her grandmother's closed bedroom door.

"No, I think I'll just sit in here for a while longer."

"Nana . . ." Dori didn't know what else to say.

Her grandfather had called first thing that morning and demanded she come over. And when Papa Bela demanded, the family responded.

So here she was, trying to cajole the most stubborn member of the family out of not just her room but her funk. And she knew she wasn't going to accomplish that standing outside her grandmother's door, so she opened it and went in.

Nana Vancy was only four feet, eleven and a half inches tall, but no one in the family seemed to notice her slight frame because her giant spirit had always eclipsed any lack in height. Now, her spirit broken, her grandmother seemed small, engulfed by the rocking chair, lost in it, Dori thought.

Just lost, period.

"Nana . . ." she started, unsure what to say.

"It's all my fault," Nana said softly. "My stupid pride brought this curse upon the family. I realized it when all my children's weddings were disasters, but with my grandchildren, it's gotten even worse. Your sister and your brother — they didn't just have disastrous weddings, they got left at the altar. And of course there was you and Leo."

"Nana, Vancy and Noah were each about to marry the wrong person," Dori patiently pointed out. "Getting left at the altar was the best thing for both of them. Now Vancy and Matt have his twin nephews with them, and they're even expecting a baby. And Noah and Callie are deliriously happy. As for Leo . . . it never got as far as talking about a wedding. It was just . . . a school thing."

"For him, maybe, but not for you, *lanyunoka*." Her grandmother shook her head. "For you it was a heartbreak. Even though you hadn't talked about a wedding, I know you'd thought about it. Apparently just a thought is enough of a curse now."

"Nana" — Dori was going to say, *You're being ridiculous,* but she knew better, so she simply said — "I'm fine. Losing Leo was for the best."

"How is having your heart broken for the best? Knowing that it was my fault, my curse, my words . . ." Her grandmother shook her head, and her gray hair swayed back and forth. "It's a burden I'll have to live with."

"Nana, they were only words. Not a curse. Just words you said in pain a long time ago."

"And anger," her grandmother said with honesty. "I thought my Bela had left me at the altar, and though I was crushed, I was also furious. I was Vancy Bashalde, the pride of Erdely, Hungary. My father was mayor. I deserved the most beautiful, elaborate wedding the town had ever seen. I was so angry that Bela had shamed me. Hurt and angry, I said the words, *'I hope Bela never gets a big, beautiful wedding like this. I hope that no one in his family does.'*"

"But Papa hadn't left you. He'd had an accident, and when he made it home, you got married and —"

"And no one in our family has ever managed that big, beautiful wedding." Nana Vancy sighed. "Even before your grandfather came back, I tried to soften the curse by adding that it wasn't future marriages I was trying to curse, just the weddings. And when a couple realized that the marriage

10

was more important than the wedding, the curse would be broken. Both Vancy and Noah let me down."

"Nana, I want the kind of love you and Papa have. The kind Mom and Dad, Vancy and Matt, and Noah and Callie have. I want a man who likes the same things I do. Someone who loves to fish and watch sunsets on the peninsula. Someone who won't want to fight with me. Who won't mind that I don't like to dress up and be a girly girl. Someone who wants me the way I am because he loves me that way. When I find him" — she didn't say *if I find him* out loud but she thought it — "I won't care about how we get married, as long as I get to spend the rest of my life with him."

In Dori's mind, finding that man, that perfect man, was probably not in the cards. It was a matter of statistics. Everyone in her family had found his or her perfect mate, so what were the odds she would do the same?

Slim to nil.

She'd learned that perfect men tended to want perfect women, and in their minds she was anything but. So Dori had long since decided that she was going to be the family's resident spinster. She'd spoil her nieces and nephews horribly and live a contented, solitary life.

She didn't need a man, and she'd given up looking.

Oh, she occasionally dated, but she never dated any man more than three times. Reporting that she was dating someone kept Nana off her back and hopeful.

But it had been a long time since Dori's last date. Given Nana's mood, she'd probably have to go out sometime soon.

Despite the fact that she never planned to marry, her words perked her grandmother up. Some of Nana's usual spirit glimmered in her eyes. "You won't care about the wedding? You promise?"

"Nana, you know me. I'm more at home in a hard hat than a frilly dress. It's an easy promise to make." Her grandmother waited. "Okay, I promise. When I decide to marry, I won't give a flying fig about the wedding."

"Well, then, get out there and find your man, Dori Salo, because I mean to see this curse broken soon."

Dori nodded at her grandmother, even as she crossed her fingers behind her back.

Dori Salo was a true believer in happily-ever-afters . . . for everyone but herself.

CHAPTER ONE

"Bill, this is a matter of life and death."

Bill Hastings didn't even bother to reply. He merely quirked an eyebrow at his overly dramatic cousin. He'd worked hard to develop that expression over the years. Sometimes it even got his cousin to calm down. Not always, but sometimes.

This was one of those times. Cecilia Hastings sighed and took a deep breath before continuing. "Okay, so maybe not life and death in a personal way, but in a business sense, it definitely is."

"Come on, CeCe."

CeCe placed her folded hands on her stomach and waited, looking every inch the fragile mother-to-be. She was very blond, very fair . . . and very pregnant. She was propped up in her bed, wearing a frilly bathrobe, and her crystal blue eyes looked watery, as if they were filled with tears.

"Bill, I wouldn't ask, but I can't risk the baby."

She'd played the baby card.

There was no way to win against the baby card.

Bill and CeCe came from a family of under-reproductive women, who'd each only managed to produce an only child. His mother and aunt were the first siblings in the Erikson family line in generations. Maybe that's why his mom and aunt were closer than most sisters. They'd married the Hastings brothers the same month, and the two couples had promptly bought houses next door to each other.

For five years his mom and his aunt had each tried to conceive. They'd both finally succeeded the same month and had raised their children more like siblings than cousins. He and CeCe had been mistaken for brother and sister more often than not. They both had their mothers' fair hair, though Bill had inherited his father's darker complexion.

Bill had spent his life running from his mom's Harrisburg house to his aunt and uncle's and back, equally at home in either.

It had been the same with CeCe.

His mother had never seemed resentful that her sister had gotten the good brother.

His own father had left when Bill was five, and Bill rarely, if ever, saw him. His Uncle John had stepped in and done his best to be a father to him, and as far as Bill was concerned, he'd succeeded.

Bill and CeCe had both gone to college in Pittsburgh. Afterward CeCe had moved to Erie and worked for an interior designer. She'd opened her own place last year.

The fact that CeCe had accidently become pregnant was a shock to the whole pregnancy-impaired family. Seeing her in bed, looking so scared and pale, Bill knew he'd do whatever she asked.

So when she played the baby card, he realized he'd lost the argument.

"The doctor said complete bed rest for the rest of the pregnancy."

"I know, CeCe. And I sympathize, but I still don't see how I can help. You're an interior designer. I'm an architect. There's no way I can take on this account for you."

Her hands were folded gently over her gigantic baby-bump, and she offered him a Madonna-ish smile. "You see, that's the beauty of it. You won't really be taking anything on. Bill, I know you've put off your life to come help me out through the last month or so of this pregnancy, and I appreciate that. And I know that I don't have

15

any right to ask you to do more. But I am. I'm asking, Bill. I want you to pretend to be my associate. You can certainly handle the presentation. I have the sketches and plans all ready to go. It's not all that different from the presentations you make as an architect."

"CeCe —" he started to protest.

She interrupted. "I just need you to go in, take the meeting, land me this job, and then I'll do the rest. Designing the interior of Salo Construction's new development's model house would be a feather in the cap of Hastings Designs, and I need the company to succeed. I mean, it's especially important now that I'm about to be a mother. The Hazard Hills development would put me on the design map."

Damn. There she went, playing that baby card again. Two times. That was no fair.

"A *single* mother, no less," she threw in for good measure.

Two baby cards and a my-boyfriend-ditched-me card? It was a winning hand.

Bill knew it but felt he had to try to bluff his way out.

"CeCe." That was all he said, just her name, because he couldn't think of a viable argument. No ace in the hole to play. He arched an eyebrow for good measure, hoping beyond all hope that it worked its

16

eyebrow magic.

It didn't.

The eyebrow card obviously wasn't nearly a strong enough hand to beat a baby and a single mother.

CeCe knew it. He could see it in the satisfied smirk she hid so expertly underneath her Madonna smile. "You already quit your job in Pittsburgh, and you said you wanted to start your own architectural firm somewhere out west, so it's not as if you're planning on staying in Erie. No one will connect Carter William Hastings the fourth with Bill Hastings, the new, up-and-coming Arizona architect. It might mean delaying your plans for a month or two, but, Bill . . ." She patted her huge stomach.

It was all over. Bill finally admitted that to himself.

To be honest, it had been over the moment CeCe asked. They'd both migrated from Harriburg, Pennsylvania, to Pittsburgh for school; then CeCe had come to Erie, and Bill had landed a position with a Pittsburgh architectural firm.

It was nice having family just two hours away. He frequently drove up for the weekend to visit CeCe.

When he'd quit the firm and sold his place, he'd come to stay with her and help her out while he tried to decide where to start his own architectural firm.

He was leaning toward Arizona. There was a big building boom. Warm climate.

Yes, Arizona looked good.

But CeCe was right. Arizona would still be there in a month or so. He could stay, help her out, and see the baby born.

"Fine," he capitulated. "But what's with using my full name?" He hated that he was named after his father, another man who was able to walk away from his responsibilities.

"Do you really think anyone will take a jeans-wearing, flannel-shirt-favoring Bill Hastings seriously as an interior designer? But a change of outfit, and boom — Carter Hastings the fourth, metrosexual interior designer extraordinaire. That Carter, he's a very serious interior designer who's come to work for Hastings Design."

Bill groaned even as CeCe grinned.

"Promise me," she said.

"CeCe . . ."

"Promise."

His cousin knew how seriously he took his promises. Bill had spent his adult life trying to be the opposite of his father. Carter William Hastings III had never met a promise he couldn't break. Bill had never knowingly broken a pledge.

CeCe waited, watching him intently.

"Fine, I promise."

She smiled and patted her stomach again. "Don't you worry. Mommy's business is fine now. Once Uncle Bill makes a promise, he never breaks it. So we'll just hang out and wait in this bed until you're ready to be born, while Uncle Bill rides to the rescue and saves the day."

CeCe had always been full of big ideas. Her idea to toilet-paper the principal's yard was the reason he'd spent the entire second half of his eighth-grade year in detention.

That was the problem with CeCe's ideas. She always made them seem almost logical.

Almost.

And every time he went along with one of her plans, it ended up biting him in the butt.

What on earth had he gotten himself into?

He had a feeling that this time the bite had the potential to be sharper than anything he'd yet experienced.

"It will be fine, Bill," CeCe said, as if she'd read his mind.

She could say that all she wanted, but Bill still had a nagging feeling that this big plan of CeCe's was going to be his downfall.

He was an architect. What did he know about impersonating an interior designer?

19

■ ■ ■ ■

Dori Salo wiped the sweat from her brow. It had been the hottest July in years. One of the hottest she remembered. Which made construction a very hot occupation.

But it was still satisfying work.

She surveyed the shell of a house and the work crew diligently plugging away at it despite the heat.

A feeling of utter contentment and satisfaction crept over her. This was her baby. Right now it was an ugly, unfinished baby, but it was coming along.

She glanced out over the bluff at the bay. Oh, yes, it was going to be a beautiful house, with the most amazing views.

Soon.

Very soon.

After years of working for the family business, Salo Construction, and representing them in the field, she'd finally gotten them to agree to contribute their efforts to Hazard Hills.

Anywhere else in the country, a subdivision with *Hazard* in its name might be frowned upon. But here in Erie, people took Oliver Hazard Perry and his role in the Battle of Lake Erie seriously. Which made

Hazard Hills the perfect name for her small development on premium bayfront property.

She'd invested a huge chunk of the business's money in purchasing the property. The factory that had occupied the site for years was finally given sufficient incentive to move and allow its property to be developed, completing the bayfront's transition from an industrial area to a hot-ticket residential and tourism area. She'd gotten a zoning permit to put up twelve houses.

This first one was to be her model home. Dori had planned every part of it herself, endlessly browbeating the architect into giving her what she envisioned. It was built of glass and stone, or at least it would be when it was finished. Her goal was to make it appear as if the house grew out of the cliff overlooking the bay. She wanted it to feel as if it had always been here.

Because it was a model, she wanted to dress it out, set the stage. For that, she needed help. Speaking of help, where on earth was the interior designer?

Cecilia Hastings was, according to friends, an up-and-coming interior designer. Having looked at a number of rooms the woman had designed, Dori agreed. She was eager to see what Hastings had come up with for

Hazard Hills' first home.

She glanced at her watch, then swiped at her brow again and wiped the sweat from the back of her hand onto her jeans.

Where was the woman?

Punctuality was important in Dori's book, and this Cecilia was losing points with every minute that ticked by.

She watched as a Honda Civic pulled up on the newly asphalted road, Lawrence Lane, in front of the house. It was practically silent — a hybrid. A man wearing a business suit got out.

As he approached, Dori could tell it wasn't just any bought-off-the-rack sort of suit. The lines were too precise, the fit too perfect for that. That suit was costly. So were his shoes. She was sure there was some designer's name attached to them. A name that added hundreds of dollars to the price.

Dori tried to keep her distaste for that kind of expense from showing. Give her a pair of jeans that fit, a shirt that didn't have any holes, and her steel-toed work boots, and she was ready for the day.

"Hello," Mr. *GQ* called as he approached, picking his way from the muddy square that would someday be the front yard. He was taller than she; because she was five eight, a lot of men weren't. His hair was a sandy blond, and as he approached, she couldn't help but notice that his eyes were a brilliant blue. Sky blue. She looked overhead and decided it was pretty precisely the color in question.

"I'm looking for Ms. Salo," Sky Blue *GQ* Man said in a voice that had the faintest of rasps to it. Like Sam Elliott on a good throat-lozenge day. Dori had always had a thing for the actor, especially his voice, which might explain why her heart did a little double beat when *GQ* Man spoke.

His voice almost made her forget his expensive clothes.

Almost.

"Miss, I'm looking for Dora Salo," he repeated.

Dori gave herself a mental shake. She'd met good-looking men before. She could handle this one. "I'm she."

He thrust out his hand. "I'm . . ." He hesitated a split second, then finished, "Carter Hastings the fourth, from Hastings Designs."

Dori shook it. Despite his pretentious name and designer clothes, he had a nice grip. "I thought I'd be meeting with Cecilia Hastings."

"My cousin. HD has had to hire more help recently. We currently have more business than Cecilia can handle alone," he offered truthfully.

"Even so, I'd expect Hazard Hills to rate a personal visit from her. Salo Construction has been an industry leader in the community for years, and I'm prepared to showcase Hastings Designs in a manner that's guaranteed to garner your company tons of exposure. I expected to be meeting with Cecilia herself," she reiterated.

Dori was not impressed with Hastings Designs thus far. And despite the man's nearly perfect voice, she didn't hold out much hope that this Carter Hastings — *the fourth,* she mentally added — was going to improve her rapidly declining opinion.

Bill could see that Dora Salo was less than pleased that he was here instead of CeCe. He decided honesty was the best policy. Well, at least some honesty.

"Ms. Salo, Cecilia is pregnant, and her doctor has put her on complete bed rest. Babies are hard to come by in our family. We each come from a long line of only children. My mother and my aunt were the first siblings in many generations. They both tried for years and finally got pregnant at the same time. CeCe and I were raised more like siblings than cousins, and I can guaran-

24

tee that she won't do anything to endanger this baby, even if it means losing a big account. Thank you for having considered Hastings Designs."

He turned and would have liked to storm off the site, but the mud and the ridiculously priced pair of shoes that CeCe had written off on HD's account as a business expense left him picking his way gingerly toward Cece's car.

He was glad this absurd deception was over as soon as it had started.

He'd promised CeCe he'd try, and Bill Hastings always kept his promises. But this was the most ludicrous one he'd ever been stuck with.

All he wanted was to go home, put on his jeans, and get back to planning his new business. What he didn't want was to spend his day kissing some prickly spinster's butt, trying to garner favor for his cousin's company.

Oh, Dora Salo was a very pretty woman, in an outdoorsy sort of way. The kind of woman he'd normally be attracted to. She had dark hair, thrown back into a casual ponytail. And she was tall, above his shoulder. At six foot even, he rarely experienced that. She had on work clothes, and she'd been sweating. It had left streaks through the dust on her face, which only made her dark brown eyes stand out all the more.

Maybe some men wouldn't care for her careless, I've-been-working style, but he liked a woman who could hold her own.

Yes, Dora Salo was attractive, but he was still glad the ruse was over before it had truly begun.

His only regret was that CeCe was going to be hugely disappointed. She so wanted this account.

Well, at least she thought she did. She hadn't met the prickly Ms. Salo.

He couldn't imagine that working with her would be a pleasurable experience. CeCe was talented, and he was sure HD could make it without the royal Salo family nod of approval.

"Wait!" Dora Salo called as he picked his way through the mud.

He kept walking, ignoring her regal, obey-me-or-off-with-your-head summons.

"Mr. Hastings!" she called again. "Please, wait."

It was the *please* that did it. He turned around and, rather than picking his way back across the construction site, waited for her to come to him. "Yes?"

"I'm sorry. Family always comes first, and babies are especially important. My sister is pregnant now too, and I know I'd do whatever had to be done to keep her and the baby safe and healthy. I'm sure if Cecilia sent you, you're more than qualified for this job. So, please, why don't you come in and take a look at the space?"

He felt like a heel about her being sure he was qualified for this particular job, because he was anything but. Yet he didn't say word. He simply nodded and allowed her to lead the way back across the mire that would someday be a front lawn.

She paused at the boards that served as a walkway to the front entrance. They spanned the space that would someday be a porch and now was just a pit. "I'm sorry about the state of the site. Can you make it across the boards?"

"Certainly," he assured her. He was at home on a construction site because he believed that an architect's job didn't stop with a set of plans. He liked to visit and make sure those plans were working, to be on hand to suggest changes if they were warranted. So he was quite at home walking across boards and navigating a working job-site.

But he was used to doing that while he was wearing proper work clothes, and, more important, proper work boots of the nice, well-tractioned, steel-toed variety.

Not some slip-on loafers with an odd little tassel dangling smartly in the center. Loafers with a flat leather bottom. A flat leather bottom that provided no traction at all, especially when coated with a layer of construction-site mud.

He made it halfway up the improvised ramp before the slipping got serious and turned into full-out sliding.

Once he started, he couldn't stop. Even worse, he couldn't steer. Which meant, rather than sliding straight down the ramp, he ended up veering to the right and running out of board. The only place left to go after that was down.

Straight down.

He landed with a thud in the bottom of the pit that would someday hold the front porch's foundation. And, due to the rain they'd have of late and the high clay content in the soil, a couple inches of water in the pit cushioned his fall.

He sat stunned and sopping at the bottom of the pit.

Then he heard it.

It was soft at first but gradually gained volume and momentum.

It was Dora Salo, laughing.

He looked up and glared.

She had the good sense to look embarrassed. "I'm so sorry, but I couldn't help it. You do make quite the picture."

He glanced down at the designer suit CeCe had insisted he couldn't live without and the stupid, tasseled, no-traction, named-after-someone shoes and had to admit that he must make quite the picture.

"No problem." He stood and tried to wipe the mud off his pants. He was pretty sure it wasn't working.

"Are you sure you're okay?" she asked between muffled giggles.

Her laughter was contagious. Bill chuckled as well. "I think I may have dented my dignity a bit."

"Hang on, and I'll help you out."

"I'll be fine."

"Did you ever read *Mike Mulligan and the Steam Shovel*?" Dora asked.

He shook his head.

"I won't comment on the sad state of your reading material, but the point was, Mike dug a basement for the new town hall so fast that he forgot to leave a way out for his steam shovel. We didn't exactly forget, but there's no way out of that hole unless you have a ladder. So hang tight, and I'll go get one."

There was nothing left for Bill to do but

wait. He tried again to brush the larger chunks of clay and mud off himself, but he wasn't sure he really succeeded.

"Here you go," Dora called, lowering a ladder to him. "Be careful climbing up. I'll bet your shoes are even slippier now that they're wet."

"Yeah, I bet they are," he muttered to himself as he climbed slowly, trying to stave off any more accidents. "Thanks," he said when he reached the top.

Dora's eyes were crinkled from her effort not to laugh. It was a valiant attempt, but she wasn't a good enough actress to manage it.

"Go ahead. I appreciate the effort, but I'm man enough to take it," he finally said.

She burst out laughing. Not some girly little giggle, but a full-out, from-the-gut laugh. Despite himself, he smiled, then laughed as well. "So, are you worried about my tracking mud into the house, or do I get the tour?"

"Come on in. Why don't we walk the boards together? You can balance yourself by holding on to my shoulders."

Part of him wanted to tell Dora Salo that he didn't need her help. That's the part that would have come to the forefront a few minutes ago, before he fell so ignominiously onto his pride. The rather dented, muddy part simply said, "That sounds like a good idea."

Slowly they made their way across the boards and into what would someday be a grand entryway but for now was an array studded walls with bits of wiring showing through on one side, insulation backing on the other.

"Can you see it?" she asked.

"Yes." He stood and appreciated the space. "Why the straight staircase?" he asked. "If you'd done this . . ." He leaned over and in the dust on the floor traced a curved stairway that followed the lines of the room. ". . . you'd be capitalizing on the space instead of chopping it up."

Dori bent over and studied his crude drawing, then looked up at the roughed-in stairway. "Yes, I like it."

They walked through the house, studying each room. She asked his decorating advice and tried to describe what she wanted. He'd turned on his PDA's recorder, so he knew he'd get the details right for CeCe.

He wasn't able to offer any further advice, so he settled for saying, time and again, "Yes, I see what you're trying for."

"And this," she said, throwing open an imaginary door, "is why I love this bluff."

31

They walked to the windows on the far side of the room, and Bill drew in his breath.

There, in full glory, was Lake Erie's bay. The dock was just barely in view to the right. Boats dotted the water directly in front of the house. A rocky cliff led down to the shoreline. Bill couldn't help but appreciate the aesthetics. "It is perfect. I can see why you wanted to build here."

"It's a Salo Construction project, but in reality, it's my baby. There've been headaches — some big ones — but I think the development will sell like hotcakes. It's not going to be huge, by some standards, but the twelve lots are in a premier spot."

"I agree."

She glanced at her watch. "Oh, I'm going to be late. Do you have enough to come up with some preliminary sketches for me? This house is to be our showcase, the development's crown jewel. Rather than build all the houses, then sell them, I wanted to get the owners in on the ground floor, so they'd have input. I want this one to be perfect."

"I think I've got enough. I want you to know that CeCe will be working with me on this project. Or, rather, I'll be working with her. Hastings Designs will throw all our resources at this one. Hazard Hills would be a great way to showcase our designs to Erie, and we appreciate your giving us a chance."

"Good. I'm glad that's settled. Now, let's see if we can get you out of here without your breaking any bones."

"Thanks." They baby-stepped back down the boards, and Bill found himself on solid ground looking a lot worse for wear. "I'll be in touch."

"Good. I can't wait to see what you come up with."

"Oh, do you have a spec sheet?" he asked.

"Sure do." She reached into a case that was sitting on some masonry blocks. "Here you go."

"Thanks."

She glanced at her watch again, gathered up her things, and took off across the muddy yard at a lope, while Bill gingerly trudged along at a snail's pace, trying to forestall another fall.

Dora Salo reached her truck, turned back, and waved before she got in and sped away.

Bill reached CeCe's tiny Civic. She'd insisted he take it, claiming no designer worth her salt would drive his battered old Ford F150 truck.

Bill wondered what his cousin would have to say when she found the mud and clay he was sure to shed all over the car's leather interior.

Whatever it was, it served her right for making him come out dressed like some Fortune 500 power broker.

By the time he drove back to CeCe's small east Erie home, he was fuming. He kicked his disgusting loafers off on the porch, let himself in, and, rather than heading straight to the guest room he was occupying, walked back to her room. He knocked.

"Come on in."

He opened the door to find CeCe, looking all Madonna-like, propped up in her bed.

Part of him wanted to ask how she was feeling, but he'd be setting himself up for her playing the baby card again, so instead he served his opening volley. "You know, CeCe Hastings, you've gotten me into some crazy situations over the years, but this one takes the cake. It even beats out the fact that you had me taking two separate girls to our senior prom."

She sat, wide-eyed, staring at him. And if he wasn't mistaken, he saw the tell tale tension that came from her trying not to laugh. "Uh, Bill, what on earth happened to you?"

Two women laughing at him in one day was two too many.

He quirked an eyebrow, and CeCe got

herself under control. He was relieved that his eyebrow still had its magic.

"Seriously," she said, all trace of laughter evaporating, "what happened?"

"Talk about a comedy of errors." He probably should have sat, given the length of his explanation, but because of the state of his clothing, he chose to stand as he outlined the entire meeting, including the part where he ended up sitting at the bottom of the soon-to-be porch.

"I think, at the beginning of the meeting, I had her convinced that your sending me instead of going yourself wasn't a slight, but, CeCe, I'm pretty sure that by the end of the meeting, she thought I was the most inept designer ever, and she's rethinking whether or not she wants to work with you."

"I'll call her."

"Good idea. And tell her the truth. She knows you're laid up in bed. She'll understand that I'm an architect who's helping out his cousin. I don't need to masquerade as an interior designer. I have no idea what prompted this crazy business, but let's just stop it."

"You promised," she reminded him. "And I refuse to capitalize on this pregnancy. If I get the job, it will be on my own merits, not some sympathy thing. I also want Dora Salo to believe that Hastings Designs has enough going for it to employ two designers. I want her to know that my work is solid, even if I am temporarily laid up. If she's dealing with you, thinking you're doing the designs and I'm just supervising, then they'll be accepted on their own merit, no sympathy involved in her decision."

"Dora Salo doesn't strike me as the type of woman to hire someone out of sympathy."

"I won't take that chance."

"Just like you won't tell the baby's father?"

"If he loved me, he'd be here. I won't have him rushing back out of pity either."

"You know, CeCe, things would be easier if you weren't so damned proud."

"You know, Bill, things would be easier on you" — she paused and grinned — "if you took a shower. I think you've ruined that suit."

"It's just mud. I'm thinking the dry cleaner will be able to fix it. But the shoes are a total wash. They're trashed. Not that I'd have worn them again if they weren't. Now I know why I stick to work boots or sneakers."

"You did look nice when you left," CeCe assured him. "I'll have to order you a new suit and shoes."

"CeCe, come on."

36

"Would you deny your pregnant cousin?"

He sighed. "You know, eventually you will give birth, and I will get even."

"I'm not due until August, so I've got leeway. A lot can happen in six or so weeks."

Bill gave up. There was nothing he could do about his crazy, pregnant cousin.

Just like there was nothing he could do about Dora Salo's opinion of him. That was what bothered him the most, and he wasn't sure why.

CHAPTER TWO

"Dora Lee Salo, you open this door." There was more loud banging on Dori's front door. "I know you're in there," her grandmother yelled.

Dori did not want to open the door.

Oh, she loved and adored Nana Vancy, but ever since Noah's wedding, Nana had been . . . well, just a little more nuts than usual.

And Nana's usual brand of nuttiness was worse than most people's, so more of it was bad news. Especially for Dori.

Dori might have coaxed Nana out of her funk at Papa Bela's insistence, but Nana had clung to the idea of Dori's breaking the curse and had become . . . well, *pest* was a strong word. But a bit of a pain. And Dori wasn't up to dealing with her grandmother's particular brand of craziness today.

Yet cowering in her house wasn't her style either.

Carter Hastings IV — la-de-da — was coming here for a meeting soon. Of course, a man who wore designer clothes to a construction site, then ended up sitting at the bottom of a pit in the mud, didn't have much room to criticize, even if he did find her huddled in the house hiding from her grandmother. Yet Dori couldn't bring herself to allow it.

She'd have to let Hastings in, and if Nana were still outside, she'd know Dori had been hiding. So, facing the inevitable, she opened the front door to her tiny grandmother. Four feet tall with snow white hair, she had an iron will — a will that was now bent on Dori's finding someone and marrying him as soon as possible.

Forcing herself to smile and praying Nana was here only to invite her to a family dinner that weekend, Dori said, "Hi, Nana."

"Don't 'Hi, Nana' me, Dora Lee Salo."

"I always know I'm in trouble when you use my full name."

"Yes, you are. And if you don't invite me in soon, you'll be in even more trouble."

"Sorry. Come on in, Nana."

Nana stomped into the living room and made herself at home on Dori's sofa.

With nothing left to do but follow, Dori took the recliner opposite the couch. "So, what brings you out so early this morning?"

"You've been avoiding me."

Dori thought about clutching at her chest and really putting on an act, but she opted to be a little less melodramatic in hopes of selling her performance. "Nana, that hurts. Really hurts. You know I'd never avoid you. I mean, what reason could I have? You're my grandmother, and I love you."

She tried to work up a tear but couldn't quite manage it. Though she doubted even tears would help. Her grandmother looked quite grim.

"Dori, I left you a message telling you I was going to fix you up on a blind date — *that's* the reason you're avoiding me."

"Nana, I —"

There were moments in everyone's life when fate saved the day, but in this case Dori suspected that the chiming of the doorbell had more to do with Carter's timely arrival than fate. Still, she'd take whatever reprieve she could get.

"Pardon me, Nana. I wouldn't want to leave someone waiting at the door." She practically bolted from the room and opened the front door again, this time to find it was indeed Carter Hastings, wearing another designer suit.

An idea came to mind. It was wicked, but

what did she have to lose?

"Carter, if you have any crazy relatives of your own, or simply any compassion at all, you'll play along with me when we walk back into my living room. Just follow my lead."

Before the man had a chance to ask any questions, she grabbed his hand and pulled him into the living room. "Nana, this is Carter Hastings. He's here to pick me up for our date."

"Date?" Her grandmother eyed Carter suspiciously. "He doesn't look like a Carter," she said. "What's your name again?"

"Carter William Hastings — the fourth," he said.

"And he's taking me out to lunch, right, Carter?"

Carter hesitated a moment, as if he wasn't quite sure she was talking to him. "Lunch. Yeah. Right. We had a date."

"And he's going like that, while you're dressed in those?"

Dori had already noted Carter's suit. What she hadn't paid any attention to were the worn jeans and T-shirt she was wearing. She laughed. "Of course not. I was just getting ready to change, when you came to the door, Nana. If you'll pardon me, I'll go change now."

Dori was generally quick to change out of a dress, but this was the first time in her life that she put one on as fast. After the light sundress was in place, she ripped her ponytail holder out and ran a brush through her hair as she stepped into a pair of sandals. A light touch of liner and mascara, and she was done.

She raced back out to the living room, where Nana and Carter were chatting like long-lost best friends. "Well, *lanyunoka,* I'll let you and this very nice boy go out to your lunch."

"Let me see you to your car, Mrs. Salo." Carter offered her grandmother his arm.

Nana looked delighted as she slipped her arm into his. "Oh, he's a nice one, Dori."

"I'm back to Dori now? No more Dora Lee?" she asked as she followed her grandmother and Carter.

Her grandmother looked at Carter, then back at Dori, and smiled. "Yes, you are. No more Dora Lee for now, though I can't guarantee how long that will last." Nana turned to Carter and said in a stage whisper, "She was always into trouble, that one."

Carter glanced back at Dori and grinned. "I can believe that."

Her grandmother looked so very happy, Dori felt a stab of guilt. "Nana, I should probably admit —"

"That she's crazy about me," Carter filled in, stopping her confession in its tracks. "But it's okay. I'm crazy about her as well."

"So, how long have the two of you been dating?"

"Mrs. Salo, I have to admit, things between Dori and me are moving fast, but it feels as if I've known her forever."

"That's how it is with the Salos," Nana told Carter. "Why, Dori's sister, Vancy, and her husband, Matt Wilde, as well as Dori's brother, Noah, and his wife, Callie, all married fast."

"Nana, Carter and I are just dating. There's not even a glimmer of a thought of marriage," Dori warned.

They'd reached her grandmother's car. Carter helped her in, then shut the door.

Her grandmother opened the window. "Thank you, young man. And, Dori, that's just what your siblings would have said if we'd asked them. And look how that turned out for both of them. Why, I'm about to become a great-grandmother again. I count Chris and Rick as mine, and soon this new baby. But you know me, I'm greedy. I'd like more."

So much for subtle, Dori thought. She was thankful she and Carter weren't really dating, because, if they were, she'd be mortified right now. "Good-bye, Nana."

"You two have a great lunch. And don't do anything I wouldn't do." She rolled up her window and backed out of the drive.

"I may have just met your grandmother," Carter said, "but I think that last bit gives us a lot of leeway."

Dori laughed. "You're right. Why don't we go back into the house, and you can show me your preliminary plans?"

"Or, since you've already changed, I could take you out to that lunch, you could explain what just happened, and then I can show you the plans."

Dori hesitated, then nodded. "That sounds like a lovely idea. Well, the lunch and the plans part anyway. The explanation is anything but lovely." As a matter of fact, her explanation was bound to sound totally crazy.

But, given her family tree, crazy was to be expected.

Dora Salo — *Dori,* Bill corrected himself — looked as uncomfortable in her sundress as he felt in his suit.

He drove downtown to State Street and parked in front of Mad Anthony's. It was one of the newer restaurants in the area,

44

and he'd eaten there once and liked it. There was an outdoor dining area. He nodded toward it as they waited to be seated. "Outside okay with you?"

Dori nodded. "I always prefer being outdoors when I can."

"Great." They got situated at a table, studied the menus, and ordered.

Bill unbuttoned the jacket to his suit and immediately regretted it. CeCe had insisted he wear a plum-colored shirt and matching tie. Unbuttoning the jacket exposed more of the jarring color. He needed to distract himself, so he looked at Dori and said, "So, spill."

"It's sort of complex. You see, my grandmother believes she put a curse on the family, and she feels I'm her last, best hope of removing it."

"A curse?"

"It'll sound crazy, no matter how I try to spin it."

"I can do crazy," Bill assured her. He was CeCe's cousin, so he'd had lots of practice.

Dori shook her head and started. "Back in Hungary, my grandfather didn't make it to their wedding on time. Nana Vancy thought he'd left her at the altar, when really he'd been in an accident and was simply delayed. Anyway, she cursed him and all his

45

heirs — that none of them would ever have a big, beautiful wedding like the wedding she didn't get — until the marriage itself meant more than the wedding. Then and only then would the curse be broken."

"And she believes that?"

Dori nodded. "When Papa Bela did show up, they didn't wait to plan another wedding — they just got married in front of the parish priest and their families. All of their children — my parents, aunts, and uncles — have had wedding mishaps. Fortunately for them, my aunts and uncles all live out of town. My father was the only one who stayed to work in the family business. My cousins are lucky that they don't have to deal with this."

"But the other side of that coin is they don't get to have such an active part in your grandparents' lives."

"Yeah, there is that. But sometimes I wish my grandparents were just a little *less* active in mine."

Bill laughed. "As for the curse, I think every wedding has its share of mishaps. Come on, how bad could it be?"

"How bad?" Dori shook her head again. "I don't believe in curses, but even I have to admit, I can understand how someone might after the list of mishaps in my family's weddings. Lightning strikes, boats that sank . . . And it only seems to be getting worse. Nana hoped to break the curse with my sister, Vancy's, wedding, but Vancy got left at the altar, then ended up marrying Matt Wilde and his twin nephews."

"She married the nephews?"

Dori laughed. "No, but she and Matt are raising Chris and Rick as if they're their own. She's pregnant now as well. After that, Nana hoped my brother, Noah's, wedding would end the curse. . . ."

"Let me guess — he eloped?"

She shook her head. "Well, no. He got jilted right before the wedding, took the bride's stepsister on the honeymoon, and fell in love. *They* eloped."

"So that leaves you?"

"Yes." The waiter brought their drinks and appetizers. Dori waited until he was gone, then continued. "Nana came over to try to fix me up with yet another blind date, but you arrived just in time."

"And I became your decoy." Bill thought CeCe had crazy down to a science, but it looked as if Dori's grandmother might have his cousin beat.

Dori nodded. "I couldn't think of anything else to do. I hope you don't mind. I know it was crazy. Really, I do know that. But you'd have to know my family to realize that crazy is our normal state of mind."

Bill took a long sip of his iced tea, then broke the news. "Well, I guess I'll have a chance to discover that for myself on Saturday."

"What's going on Saturday?" Dori asked.

"A picnic at your grandmother's, or so rumor has it. And I was not merely invited — it was more of a royal decree. I *will* be attending, I was told."

"Oh, Carter. What have I done?"

Bill was getting pretty good at charades. Dori Salo actually believed he was an interior designer named Carter. If he hadn't made a promise to CeCe, no matter how absurd it was, he'd confess everything right now.

Having met Dori, he was pretty sure that she'd understand. She'd admitted that her own sister was pregnant, so she'd understand his humoring CeCe. But he had made a promise, and if there was one thing he was known for, it was keeping his promises. He'd learned at an early age how important that was.

His father had broken far too many promises over the years, not just to Bill, but also to his mother. Promises to Bill that he'd come to this game or that school event.

Promises to his mother that he was done cheating on her, done drinking. Some boys longed to grow up to be just like their fathers.

Bill grew up trying to be the exact opposite.

He'd never knowingly broken a promise, and he didn't mean to start now.

So he didn't make his confession to Dori, no matter how much he wanted to. He couldn't until CeCe released him from his pledge.

"Dora, it's fine. Acting as your date for an afternoon isn't in any way a hardship."

"I guess if we're dating, you should call me Dori. Everyone else does."

"Then Dori it is." He'd been thinking of her that way since her grandmother called her that. It suited her much better than Dora did.

"Dori, since we're dating, why don't we forget the plans until after lunch and play first-date twenty-questions. That way, I can be more convincing when I meet your family."

"Are you sure?" she asked.

"Yes. So you start. Tell me more about your family."

And she did. She told him about growing up the youngest of three children.

She told him about having to fight with her brother, father, and grandfather for a place in the family business. And not a place like her sister's, who was a lawyer, but out in the field, working as one of the guys.

". . . It's taken me years to earn their respect and the respect of the men I work with. That's why Hazard Hills is so important to me. I want to do more than supervise construction sites. I want to have a hand in developing the city. I've got so many plans. This property is just the beginning. My sister-in-law, Callie, helps renovate old houses and sells them affordably to low-income, first-time home owners. I'm trying to convince my family that we can do something even bigger than that and turn a profit at it as well. Not a big profit, but enough to justify Salo Construction's doing it.

"There's an old factory just west of State on Eleventh. It used to make ceramic tile. Why not convert the factory into condos? Not plush, uber-expensive apartments, but nice, reasonably-priced homes. People could own their own apartments. It would not only revitalize the downtown area but also provide homes to people with average incomes. They can build equity instead of just paying rent."

"I think it's a great idea." Bill had liked Dori Salo from the moment he met her. But listening to her wax poetic about her plans for her family's company, and for the city, gave him a deep respect for her as well.

"That's just one of the reasons Hazard Hills is so important," she continued. "If I can make a go with it, then my family will let me try other ventures. I want the tile factory to be the next one."

"Do you have an architect in mind?"

She shook her head. "We've worked with a few over the years, but I want someone special for this. Turning an industrial space into efficient, comfortable homes and working to keep the costs down . . . well, it's going to take someone special. Someone with vision."

Bill wanted nothing more than to put his name into the hat. This was the kind of project he hoped to work on when he opened his own place. Something that required new and innovative ideas. "Green" building was one of his big passions, and he was already mentally calculating ways they could utilize some of that in an old factory. Energy efficiency, renewable energy . . .

He forced himself to stop. He was pretending to be an interior designer, not an architect.

He'd talk to CeCe as soon as he got home, and maybe she'd release him from his promise. Then he'd explain everything to Dori, and after she got done being annoyed, he'd see about wowing her with his architectural designs.

"So, what about you?" Dori asked, pulling him out of his daydream. "I sort of monopolized the conversation so far. I get a bit passionate about my projects. Tell me about your family."

"Passion isn't a bad thing." He paused, trying to decide how much he could tell her without actually lying. "There's not much to tell. We're nothing like your family."

Dori laughed. "Yeah, it's rare to find anything like my family."

"I'm an only child. As I mentioned before, my mom's family is a very under-reproductive one. The fact that she had a sister was a rarity in her family tree. My aunt had my cousin three months after I was born, and we were raised more like siblings than cousins. We lived next door to each other — my mom and my aunt still do. My dad left for good when I was five, so I spent a ton of time at my aunt's while Mom was at work, which only made my cousin and me closer."

"That's Cecilia, right?" Dori asked.

"Right."

"And now you work with her. That's nice. I do understand family businesses."

Wanting to be honest, he said, "I'm not sure how long I'll be working for Hastings Designs."

"Oh?"

"I was working in Pittsburgh and quit my job to move to Arizona. But CeCe used persuasive arguments to get me to come and work with her until after her baby's born."

"Well, I'm glad she did. If your cousin had come instead of you, I'd be stuck on a blind date with Nana's guy."

"Maybe you shouldn't thank me. Maybe he was *the one.*"

"No. I'm rather sure he wasn't. I don't know if there is a *one* for me. And even if there was, I'm not sure I'd recognize him, at least not the way Vancy and Noah recognized theirs."

"What makes you say that?" he asked. He wasn't sure why, but he really wanted to hear her answer to that particular question.

Unfortunately, Dori ignored it and said, "Well, I think we know enough about each other to convince my family we're dating. We're here for business. So show me those plans."

■ ■ ■ ■

Two hours later, Bill brought Dori's initial ideas back to CeCe. "She seemed enthused. But she is talking to other designers as well. She said we should hear soon."

"Yes, I know." CeCe had her laptop propped open but managed to flop back onto her pillows without upsetting it. "That's one of the reasons I don't want the fact that I'm laid up for a few months to get around too much. If all other things are equal, that might be enough to keep me out of the running on new projects."

"All things are never equal when you're involved."

"Thanks." She paused. "I think."

"It was a compliment. I know how good you are at what you do."

"Let's just hope Dora Salo does." CeCe leaned forward in the bed. "So tell me the rest."

"What 'rest'?" Bill shrugged and tried to look nonchalant.

"What else went on?"

He hesitated, not really wanting to share the fact that in addition to masquerading as an interior designer for her, he was also masquerading as a date for Dori. "What makes you think anything else went on?"

"Well, initially I just wondered what else she had to say about the project, but from the way you're acting, I now assume something else is indeed going on. Something you don't want to tell me. Which lets me know I definitely want to know."

He sat gingerly on the edge of her bed. "Stop doing that read-my-mind voodoo that you do so well."

"If I could read your mind, I wouldn't have to ask. But I can read you enough to know when you're acting fishy, so spill."

"CeCe —"

She cut him off. "Do you really want to upset the bedridden, pregnant woman? What do you suppose my mom would do if I called her to complain?"

"She'd call my mom."

"And what do you suppose your mom would do?" Her expression said she knew she had him.

He shook his head and tsked. "You're a cruel woman, CeCe Hastings."

"Yes, I am. Now, spill."

"It's just that there was a slight misunderstanding when I took the designs over to Dori's. Her grandmother was there, trying to fix her up with some guy because of the family wedding curse, and Dori doesn't want to be fixed up — not that I blame her — so . . . well, the long and short of it is, I'm going to Saturday brunch at her grandmother's as Dori's date."

"Bill, you do know I want the 'long' of that particular story, not the 'short' of it, right?"

Sighing, he admitted defeat, and there, on the edge of CeCe's bed, he filled her in.

"Oh, Bill, you've turned into quite the actor."

"About that — I'd like to tell Dori the truth."

Her laughter died. "No."

"But, CeCe, this is stupid." Instantly he could see that calling her concerns stupid was probably not the right path to follow.

CeCe got that stubborn look on her face, the one she used to get when he tried to talk her into something she didn't want to do. Like baseball. CeCe would never join in the neighborhood baseball games, and nothing he did ever convinced her to try.

"Bill, we're in this now. As far as Dori's concerned, you're an interior designer. A metrosexual, clothing-and-image–conscious designer. You drink bottled water and like sushi."

"I don't want . . ."

"Bill, you promised."

56

CeCe knew just where to strike.

"It's ridiculous," he maintained.

He saw the sign. That quiver of CeCe's bottom lip. A slight furrowing of her brow. From there, it went to a small, almost imperceptible sniff, followed by rapid blinking.

Bill did what any self-respecting man would do — he back-pedaled. "CeCe, I didn't mean —"

"Oh, yes, you did. Ridiculous CeCe. Cecilia Hastings, pregnant and deserted by the baby's father, the sole support of this poor child, is ridiculous to be concerned about her business, their only source of income. I mean, if Hastings Designs fails, we're destitute, and you know what that means, don't you? I'll have to move in with my mother. Yes, back to the house right next door to your mother's. And when I spend my days crying because of my failed potential, they'll say, 'CeCe darling, how did this happen?' and I'll tell them, it was because I was a ridiculous woman, ridiculous to believe that my cousin, who is closer to me than any brother could be, would support me. That he thought it was ridiculous to help me save my business and that he just quit, packed up, and moved to Arizona."

"CeCe."

"You just go confess, Bill. Ruin my reputation. I'm sure Junior will love living with his grandmother and next door to his great-aunt. Of course, I'll go quietly crazy. I'll have to go golfing with my dad in order to get a break. And you know I hate golf almost as much as I hate baseball. Each stroke I miss will be on your head, Carter William Hastings the fourth. And when I get sunburned and end up with skin cancer, you'll have to take Junior and raise him as your own. And I assure you, that will put a crimp in your dating life."

"CeCe, I give up. I surrender." He held his hands up in the universal sign of defeat. "I'm sorry I called you ridiculous, and I'll continue to play my part."

Miraculously, the tears immediately dried, and CeCe turned the laptop — which was still propped on her legs — around so he could see it. "Good, because I ordered you a couple more suits. And since you're going to a picnic" — she flipped the computer back her way and started typing — "I'll have to get in a rush order for a more casual outfit. We want the Salos to be impressed."

Nothing in Bill wanted to continue with this farce, but, given his cousin's fragile emotional state, he couldn't see a way out of it.

He wished he could get his hands on the baby's father. He should be here, supporting her. What kind of guy walked out on the mother of his child?

With all his trips to visit CeCe in Erie, he'd never met the guy. She'd never even mentioned she was dating anyone, and she refused to tell him anything about the man.

The baby's father wasn't here, and Bill was. And if that meant playing out a ridiculous charade for CeCe's benefit, so be it. For now, he was Carter Hastings, metrosexual interior designer.

But as soon as she had that baby, he was done. He was going to get out of town, move to Arizona, and open his own firm.

Until then, he would be an actor extraordinaire. Pretending to be CeCe's partner and Dori's date.

For some reason, standing in as Dori's date wasn't nearly as upsetting to him as pretending to be CeCe's partner.

He wasn't sure why.

CHAPTER THREE

Saturday dinners at Nana Vancy's were nothing new. The whole family managed to get together for them at least once a month, usually even more frequently. So Dori wasn't quite sure why she was so nervous about today's picnic.

She'd changed her clothes at least a dozen times.

That was definitely not like her.

Normally a pair of jeans and a polo shirt sufficed. And she would forgo her steel-toed work boots in favor of a pair of sneakers.

She tried not to wonder too much why today was different, why it mattered to her how she looked.

And she definitely wasn't going to consider why she not only used some eyeliner but pulled out the mascara she'd bought for Noah's stag party and ran it over her lashes.

She didn't think or consider any of it as she drove her truck to Carter Hastings' house. Carter Hastings *the fourth,* she corrected herself mentally.

She absolutely didn't consider any of it as she pulled up in front of the small east Erie home he'd given her the address of. It was a bright yellow bungalow with myriad colorful flowers out front. White wicker furniture with yellow and pink striped cushions sat on the front porch.

It was cute.

It was kind of girly.

Carter might like to dress well, but this didn't strike her as his taste.

Seriously, not any man's taste.

He shut the door behind him and came down the stairs looking very preppy in pressed tan pants and an equally pressed polo shirt.

Who ironed his polo shirts?

Dori considered polo shirts well on the way to dressing up, but she'd never considered ironing one.

Okay, so she didn't iron anything.

If it wasn't wash-and-wear, she wasn't wearing it. Her only exception to that rule was a few dry-clean-only outfits that she saved for weddings and funerals, because she didn't have to iron those.

Surely pressing a polo shirt was a sign of a very sick mind.

"Hi," Carter said as he opened the passenger door of the truck.

Man, even his shoes were shined. Or brand-new. Either way, they made her dusty old Docksiders look . . . well, dusty and old.

"Hi." Be nice, she sternly reminded herself. Just because she'd never been a *Cosmo* dresser didn't mean others couldn't take an active interest in their looks.

She glanced at Carter again.

An *over*active interest.

She forced a smile. "So, are you ready for a family gathering?"

"I hope so. I'll confess, I never thought of myself as a great actor. Well, until recently." He snapped on his seat belt.

Dori threw the truck into gear, trying to ignore the nagging feeling that this was a mistake of epic proportions.

"I appreciate your acting on my behalf. Odds are, though, they're going to doubt we have long-term dating potential anyway."

"Why would you say that?" he asked.

"Well, look at you, then look at me."

He obliged. She could almost feel his eyes boring into her, and she wished she could suck her words back in. "Okay, enough looking at me. My point is, you're . . . well, you dress like that on a daily basis, and this is from my dressy-clothes side of the closet."

"Hey, I saw you in a dress the other day. It was very nice. And it suited you."

"It wasn't really a dress, it was a sundress, and that was from my uber-dressy section. That particular section is sparse, to say the least. There's the sundress and the dresses I bought for my brother and sister's weddings. That's about it."

"So, you feel your family is so superficial that they wouldn't believe a man could be interested in you despite your wardrobe?"

She glanced at him and saw he wasn't mocking; he was genuinely curious. "No . . ."

"Oh, then you believe that just because I dress well, I couldn't be interested in you despite your wardrobe? That a man who wears good suits is too shallow for anything more than a casual relationship?"

"Come on, you're sounding insulted, and we both know you're here because you want to curry my favor for Hastings Designs."

"Stop the truck!" he practically barked.

"Pardon?"

"Stop. The. Truck."

She obliged and glided to the curb. "What?"

"Listen, Ms. Salo, I don't need to curry favor for CeCe's company by playing a gigolo to some image-impaired princess. I said I'd do this because your grandmother seemed nice, and so did you — and I'm not saying that just because of the Hazard Hills project. I really enjoyed our lunch. But I can see now, you're not the woman I thought you were. You're hung up on appearances. Since I'm not able to alter mine at present, it's best if I go now."

"Listen, Carter, I didn't mean —"

"Yes, you did. Please extend my regrets to your grandmother."

"You can't walk home from here."

"We're not that far. I can see how my choice of clothing might make you think I'm too soft to manage those six or so blocks, but I'm capable."

"I'm sorry. I mean, really sorry. I'll drive you back. It's the least I can do."

"Fine."

"Carter, I didn't mean . . ." She stopped herself. "Okay, so I did. I've found that most men are looking for something in women that I don't seem to possess. And I guess I took it out on you."

"What do you mean?" he asked.

"I'm a 'Mary Ann.' And, unfortunately, most men want a 'Ginger.' "

That's who her ex had ended up with. She'd run into him a year or so ago. His wife had *Ginger* written all over her. Maybe

64

that's why Carter's wardrobe bothered her. He seemed to be a male Ginger.

She wisely didn't voice that thought as she waited to see what he was going to say next.

After a lengthy pause, he laughed. "Wow, I think you've been hanging out with the wrong men. Listen, throw the truck back into gear, but forget turning it around. I'll go with you."

"I don't need you to come out of pity."

"And I don't need to curry favor by helping you get your grandmother off your back. Hastings Designs can win the account on its own merit."

She started once more toward her grandparents' house. "You're right. It can."

She glanced over as he cocked his head to one side and looked at her, waiting.

"I looked over your preliminary sketches, and they're good. I have a few changes I'd like to suggest, but they're very good. If you still want it, you've got the job. And it has nothing to do with this pseudo-date."

"Well, I'm pleased. And of course this is where I say, you made the right decision."

She glanced over at his grin and smiled back. "Ex-boyfriends not withstanding, I generally do."

"Good to hear. But we can discuss your

changes — and business in general — any day next week. It's Saturday. We're going to your family's gathering, and we're going to have a wonderful time."

"You do know that my grandmother is going to pester you to death, right?" she asked.

"I can handle her."

This time Dori laughed as she shook her head. "Oh, you poor, foolish man. Rose-colored glasses won't go very well with your clothes."

"I'll tell you what. If I make it through this entire picnic without a problem, I'll take you to see the secret of my success."

"What does that mean?"

"Deal?"

Dori nodded. "Deal."

He laughed again. It was a deep, raspy sound that sent a flutter of something throughout Dori's system and made her think of Sam Elliott again. She glanced at Carter. He was a boy Ginger, not a Sam. She regretted that.

She firmly tamped down her disappointment.

After all, she was a Mary Ann. Men saw her as a buddy, a pal. They didn't see her as a Ginger and never would. Even Carter Hastings IV was helping her out of . . . well, not out of any need to win her favor.

So why was Carter helping her?

She was about to ask but ran out of time to do so. They pulled up in front of her grandparents'. "Show's on."

She must not have sounded overly enthused, because Carter said, "It will all be fine, Dori."

"Yeah, fine."

She thought about offering him some tips but had no chance. Her grandmother opened the front door. "Dori, *lanyunoka,* you and your Carter are here. I'm so glad."

She beckoned them inside and gave Carter a quick hug. "I'm happy you were able to join us."

She led them into the dining room. "Now, Dora Lee, you make the introductions."

"Hold on to your hat, Carter," she said quietly, for his ears only. More loudly, she said, "Everyone, this is Carter Hastings. Carter, this is my grandfather, Bela Salo, and you already know Nana Vancy. These are my parents, Mary Jane and Emil Salo. My grandmother's namesake and my older sister, Vancy Wilde, her husband, Matt, and their boys, Chris and Rick."

As she made the last introductions, she realized how huge her sister was.

Seriously, Volkswagen Beetle round.

But despite her size, Vancy managed to

look completely happy, standing there with her arms around the boys and Matt next to her. The four of them — Vancy, Matt, and the boys — made a perfect-looking, dark-haired family. No one would ever guess that Chris and Rick were just Matt's nephews. Thinking about what a time they had had forming their family made Dori's throat get tight.

"When's the baby due?" Carter, who'd obviously also noted her sister's jumbo-ness, asked.

"Just a few more weeks," Vancy said, patting her stomach.

Dori spotted her brother and his wife walking into the dining room from the kitchen. "And that's my brother, Noah, and his wife, Callie." Noah was as tall and dark-haired as the rest of the family, but Callie was tiny, just barely over five foot, with fire engine red hair that made her stand out.

"Pleased to meet you all." Carter smiled, looking far more at ease than Dori felt. "I'll do my best to remember your names."

"Don't worry if you don't," Nana Vancy assured him. "Sometimes Bela forgets their names, and he's known them a lot longer than you."

"Don't listen to my wife," the big man said as he walked up to Carter and thrust out a huge hand.

Carter took it and shook it. "Mr. Salo."

"You can call me Bela, young man. I don't stand on formalities."

"Bela, then. I want to thank you for having me over today."

"If you're dating our Dori, then of course we're delighted to have you here." He lowered his usual booming voice and switched to a stage whisper. "The better to check you out."

"Papa, you forget, your whisper is still louder than most people's speaking voices. I heard that," Dori assured him.

"You were meant to, Dora Lee. After Vancy and Noah's ill-fated life choices, we've all decided to keep an eye on you."

"And that's a new situation, how?" She turned to Carter. "Being the baby of the family means I've always had a lot of people 'keeping an eye on me.' Remind me later to tell you about the time Noah decided he didn't like my prom date."

"How bad was the prom date?" Carter asked.

"In retrospect, the guy wasn't all that great, but I was talking about my brother. I mean, after four years of high school, I'd finally made it to our school's version of a lovers' lane, and my brother and half the football team showed up and knocked on the window. It was that bad."

Carter glanced back at Noah. "Ouch."

"Enough of that," her grandfather said. "Carter, do you know anything about the manly art of grilling meat?"

"Sir, I've had it on the best authority that I have a gift for grilling."

"Ah, a man who's not afraid to tell it like it is. Come with me, then, and I'll show you my new grill. It can cook fifty-four hot dogs at once."

"You know that how?" Dori called out as the two men walked away.

Her grandfather turned and grinned. "I counted, of course."

Her grandmother snorted. "And I didn't have to cook for a week. We just microwaved grilled hot dogs." She started toward the kitchen. "Come give us a hand, *kedvenc.*"

Dori watched Carter be engulfed by the men of her family as they stood around her grandfather's new stainless steel grill, like some ancient warrior clan worshiping at an altar.

Despite the fact that he was the only one with shiny shoes, he looked at home with them all.

"Dora Lee, those carrots won't peel themselves," her grandmother called. "Stop mooning over that boy, and come help."

Mooning? "I don't 'moon.' "

Her grandmother snorted.

Dori couldn't think of any brilliant retort, so she turned and followed her grandmother into the kitchen.

She wasn't mooning.

Well, not really.

Just admiring the view.

Nothing wrong with that.

Was there?

Bill hadn't expected to like Dori's family as much as he did.

They were the real deal. Warm, not just with each other but including him. No one commented on his being way overdressed.

He was going to kill CeCe.

It didn't take long for him to realize that CeCe was wrong, that designer clothes were not going to win over anyone in this family.

All he wanted to do was drop the pretense, get into his jeans, and introduce himself to the Salo family all over again. He felt like a fraud, not only for the way he was dressed, but for the whole charade. Because, truth be told, he genuinely liked Dori's family.

He looked at Dori talking to her very pregnant sister on the other side of the

71

patio. He felt a pang of guilt over his deception.

He should tell her the truth.

CeCe's concerns were ridiculous, but how could he get his cousin to see that? Her pregnancy was making her a little less than rational.

Okay, a lot less.

And, truth be told, CeCe was never known for her rationality to begin with. Their moms always said she had an artist's temperament.

"Matt, do you think Nana has any of those Popsicles left?" Vancy asked.

"Popsicles?" Dori asked.

Matt gave his wife an indulgent smile. "Vancy's had cravings for them." He kissed her on the forehead. "Let me go check."

Bill realized that CeCe had no one in her life to go get her Popsicles. How could her ex have walked out and left her like that?

He couldn't make up for the fact that she was going to be a single mother, but he could make things easier on his cousin. And if that meant pretending to be an interior designer, then so be it.

He was moving to Arizona as soon as he was sure CeCe and the baby were okay. The Salo family would never have to be any the wiser. And it wasn't as if he were trying to bilk them out of money or anything like that. He was just pretending to design interiors rather than buildings.

And wearing clothes he wasn't comfortable in.

The last part affected him the most at the moment. The Salos all looked comfortable in their everyday clothes, while he felt like a mall mannequin in his new, *casual,* outfit.

"Brats are bigger than hot dogs, Papa," Noah said. "I don't think you can fit over fifty on this grill and still be able to turn them."

"I think I can," the giant, gray-haired man maintained. "It's all in how you flip them."

"Nah, Papa, I'm with Noah. It's not going to happen," Callie said.

Matt came back and handed Vancy a Popsicle. "What're we talking about?"

"How many bratwursts Papa can get onto the grill," Callie told him.

"No more than forty, tops." Matt sounded decisive.

"You're all full of it," their grandfather scoffed. "Carter, boy, what do you think?"

"I'm Switzerland. No opinion." No way was he getting into the middle of this. He'd seen his aunt and mom have weird, useless arguments like this, and he knew better.

"Coward," Matt teased.

"No, just smart. Too smart to get into an argument with my date's grandfather, brother, and brother-in-law. There's no good side to pick, so I'm staying neutral."

"He's a wise man," Dori's grandfather said. "Now count 'em and weep, boys."

Bill, Matt, and Noah all started counting. "One, two, three . . ."

Dori came up beside him. "What's going on?"

Matt and Noah continued, ". . . eight, nine, ten . . ."

Bill turned and smiled at her. "They have a bet on how many bratwursts your grandfather can fit on his new grill."

". . . fifteen, sixteen, seventeen . . ."

"How many did you guess?"

"He's Switzerland," Matt told her, then rejoined Noah. ". . . twenty-one, twenty-two . . ."

"A smart man," her grandfather added.

Dori pulled him a little farther away from the men. "You're okay?"

"I'm fine. Having fun, as a matter of fact."

She didn't look as if she believed him. "Okay. If you say so. I was just checking. I know my family can be overwhelming at times."

"I'm fine, Dori."

". . . thirty-three . . ."

She lowered her voice. "You didn't sign on for this."

"Yes, I did. I've got a family too. Not as big as yours, but I knew what I was getting into."

She gave him an odd look. "Well, then, okay. I'd best go help Nana out before she comes looking for me."

". . . forty, forty-one . . ."

"Go." He rejoined the counting. ". . . forty-eight, forty-nine, fifty, fifty-one."

"That's it," their grandfather said triumphantly. "More than fifty. Now, that's some grill."

Thirty minutes later they all gathered at four picnic tables grouped under an awning at the back of the house. The brats, salads, and fresh corn weighed down the table to the point of groaning.

Dori's grandmother poured Bill a lemonade, then continued down the table, filling everyone's glass. She looped around and supplied the other side.

"Hey, Nana, Ricky got more than me," the twin — who must be Chris, if Bill was remembering correctly — complained.

Ricky didn't make any response. He just smiled as he took a long, satisfied drink.

"You finish that, and I'll get you more, *kedvenc*," Dori's grandmother promised.

"There's always enough for everyone at my house."

Chris nodded and looked satisfied as he took a drink as well.

The rest of the meal passed quickly. Family jokes and conversations leaped from one end of the table to the other, comments lobbed back and forth.

Bill felt like a spectator at a tennis match, craning his head from one direction to the other, catching bits of things he could follow and other conversations that required more family history than he currently possessed.

But what delighted him the most was when the family started sharing Dori stories.

". . . and remember that time Mom tried to make Dori wear a dress for picture day?"

Noah burst out laughing. "Oh, do I. Before you go, Carter, remind me to show you the photo. Nana Vancy has a copy hanging in the back hall."

"What happened?"

"The world will never know. All we do know is that when the package of pictures came home, there was Dori, wearing a Salo Construction T-shirt that was at least three sizes too big."

"And a hard hat," Vancy added.

"Oh, I about did her in," Dori's mom assured him, her grin belying the words.

"I told you, Mom, I don't do dresses. Didn't then, don't now."

"She had on a sundress the other day when she went out with Carter here," her grandmother supplied.

Bill tried to ignore the fact that this family he liked so very much kept calling him Carter. Only his teachers had called him that. Everyone else knew him as Bill.

In his head, his father was Carter, and he was Bill.

He brutally pushed the guilt of his ruse back into a corner and watched with delight as Dori blushed over the fact that she'd worn a sundress to their lunch.

"I didn't realize wearing dresses was so out of character for Dori. If I did, I'd have been even more appreciative," he said. Then, needing to say something to make Dori feel better, he added, "But you should do it more often. You looked lovely."

Vancy and Callie both did a breathy little "ahhh" together, and, rather than look relieved, Dori turned red.

"Could we please stop discussing me? I mean, no more old family stories that Carter doesn't need or want to hear. Let's move on to talking about Vancy and Matt's baby."

Vancy immediately warmed to the subject

and started in on baby names and her thoughts about decorating the nursery. "I want a Disney-themed room, but Matt and the boys are insisting the baby would want trucks."

"Maybe Carter could give you some ideas, something that would keep you all happy. A compromise." Dori's grandmother looked at him. "You wouldn't mind, would you, Carter?"

Dori looked as if she wanted to crawl into a hole. "Really, I'm sure Carter doesn't have time."

At the same moment Carter said, "No, of course I wouldn't mind. I'd be delighted."

"Could you come over tomorrow?" Vancy looked thrilled with the suggestion. "I know it's an imposition, but there's not much time left, so the sooner we settle on something and get started, the better."

"You're sure?" Dori asked Bill.

He nodded.

"Fine. Then I'll bring him over myself," Dori promised. Then she blushed again. "I mean, if that's all right with you, Carter."

"Yeah, that would be fine," he heard himself agreeing.

That would be fine?

What on earth was he thinking?

Coming up with something for Dori's

model house wasn't a problem; he just took the specs to CeCe and let her have at them. No way could he do that for Vancy Wilde's house. He'd be walking in cold, with no idea of what sort of room it was or what sort of designs would work as a compromise between Disney and trucks.

He had dug himself into a hole when he agreed to CeCe's crazy scheme, and the hole was growing deeper with every passing minute. And he had no idea what to do about it.

CHAPTER FOUR

"I loved the picture," Carter teased as Dori drove down Twelfth Street.

Her grandmother hadn't forgotten the conversation at dinner, and before they could make their escape, she'd come out with the picture of Dori in her too-big T-shirt and hard hat.

"No one can say I don't have a sense of timeless fashion. I mean, I still wear that same outfit today."

He laughed, which had been her intent.

"Are you going to give me any clue where we're going?"

"I promised I'd show you the secret of my success if I survived the dinner, and that's where we're going. So just turn right on Peninsula."

"It's getting late. I've kept you all day. Are you sure you have time for this?"

"Dori, if you've had enough of me and you don't want to go, we don't have to."

She immediately felt like a heel. "That's not what I meant. I just feel bad that not only did my family commandeer your entire Saturday, but they suckered you into tomorrow as well. You're going to curse the day you stumbled onto the Salo family."

She glanced over at him, and he gave her a look she couldn't quite decipher.

"I don't think that's going to happen," he assured her.

He continued to directed her.

Erie was blessed with a natural peninsula that jutted out into Lake Erie. On the east side, it formed Erie's bay. As they drove down the peninsula, Dori could make out the bustling city center to the right.

The last few years had seen tremendous growth downtown, including the new convention center and the Bicentennial Tower.

On the west, the peninsula had some of the best beaches around. "Where to?" she asked.

"Take the first turn over to the beaches."

She did, and soon they were parked. "Come on," Carter prompted. He took off his expensive-looking shoes and tan socks, then cuffed his perfectly-cuffed pants a few times.

Dori followed suit, and soon, barefoot, they walked onto the sand.

"This is the secret of your success?" she asked. The beach was almost deserted. Only a few people dotted the sand.

"Sit down, Dori."

They sat on the sand, since they hadn't brought chairs or a blanket. Carter didn't seem to mind that his pants were going to get dirty. He just smiled as he looked out at the lake. The breakwaters, just off the beach, were filled with seagulls, and the sun was sinking, almost touching the horizon.

"This is my secret."

"The sunset?"

"That's part of it. My secret is knowing what's important. Whether that's helping out a new friend by going to a family picnic or to her sister's to look at a nursery. Or helping out my cousin. Or sitting on the beach, watching a sunset. These are the things that matter. And if you get the family, friends, and occasional sunset thing right, you're a success."

"Is this the part where you tell me that when I can take the grain of rice from your hand, I'll be ready for enlightenment, master?" She smiled to let him know she was teasing.

"I think it was a pebble in the parable. And I guess this is where I admit that it's definitely been said before, and often more succinctly. Stop and smell the roses."

Dori realized Carter was right. " 'We live in deeds, not years: in thoughts, not breaths; in feelings, not in figures on a dial. We should count time by heartthrobs. He most lives who thinks most, feels the noblest, acts the best.' It's a quote by a man named David Bailey. I don't know why I remember it, but it's always stuck with me."

"I read a book once called *Wherever You Go, There You Are* by Jon Kabat-Zinn. Always loved the thought behind that title."

"Wow, we're in a deep mood tonight," Dori teased again.

She realized that she was uncomfortable. Not because of anything Carter had said, but because she sensed that he got her. They sat in silence after that, side by side, watching the sun sink lower, lower, until it touched the water, then sank below the horizon.

"That was lovely. I used to come out here all the time just for sunsets like this. But this summer I've been so busy, I haven't been out once."

"Well, you have now." He rose. "I'd better let you get back to your plans," he said as he extended a hand to help Dori up.

As she took his hand, she felt a little flutter in her stomach. A weird sort of feeling.

Maybe she was hungry?

"How about we stop at Sarah's on the way off the peninsula? I'll treat you to an ice cream," she offered.

She realized they were still holding hands. She dropped his and was thankful it was dusk, because she was pretty sure she was blushing.

"I'd like that," Carter said, as if he hadn't noticed her strange reaction.

"Good."

They walked silently back toward the truck. Dori realized that something had changed between them, and she wasn't sure what it was.

But she refused to think too hard about it.

Bill was in a fine state by the time Dori dropped him off at CeCe's bright yellow house. He let himself in and stormed to her bedroom.

The door was open, so he walked right in and without preamble said, "I know you're my cousin and that you're as close as any sister could be —"

"Well, thanks, Bill. That's sweet. And believe me, I could use some sweetness today. The baby hasn't stopped kicking. I've been trying to work on the Salo plans. I had this great idea —"

"Don't you want to know why I'm re-minding myself that you're my cousin but I love you like a sister?"

She paused. "No, I don't think I do. Because we're close and I recognize that particular expression, let me rephrase that. I'm *sure* I don't want to know why you have to remind yourself."

"Ask me where I'm going tomorrow." He flopped into the chair next to her bed.

CeCe shook her head, but he continued staring at her, waiting.

Finally she asked, "Where?"

"Dori's sister's house."

"Oh, that's nice. They must like you."

"No. They like Carter William Hastings the fourth. Your metrosexual-interior-designer creation."

"Now, Bill —"

"And here's the problem," he admitted. "I want them to like me. To like Bill Hastings, architect and cousin to the crazy, pregnant interior designer, CeCe Hastings."

Finally CeCe seemed to get how serious he was. She looked concerned. "What's going on, Bill?"

"I like her." There. He'd admitted it. Not only to himself, but to CeCe.

"Her who?"

"Don't do that. Don't act as if this baby

85

growing inside you has in any way decreased your intelligence — or mine, for that matter. I like Dori, CeCe. I like her family as well, but what I feel for her is . . . well, more. It took everything I had not to kiss her good night. But she'd have been kissing Carter. And the problem is, I want her to kiss Bill."

"You know, you've always thought too much, Bill. My mother and your mother always said so, and I'm saying it now as well. You're making this a problem, and it's not."

"CeCe —"

This time she cut him off. "No. Let's look at the facts. Fact one." She held up an index finger. "You're both Bill and Carter. The only difference is, Carter dresses better."

"That and he's an interior designer, not an architect," Bill reminded her.

"Those aren't such big differences. After all, one envisions the interior design, the other the structure, but they're both creative jobs."

She held up her index and middle fingers. "Number two. Being Carter doesn't mean you can't kiss Dori. But whether you're Carter or Bill, before you get involved with someone, you need to be sure she understands that you're leaving town as soon as I'm on my feet."

"But —"

"Third" — her ring finger shot up and joined the other two — "let's not forget, since you are leaving as soon as I'm on my feet, it's not as if you're going to keep bumping into these people."

"You're right." He was leaving Erie. Ultimately, the feelings he had for Dori didn't matter, because soon he'd be gone.

"You are still leaving?" she asked.

He nodded. "Yes. I have a plan."

"And everyone knows that when Carter William Hastings the fourth has a plan, he sticks to it."

"Yes, everyone knows that." And for the first time, he found himself almost regretting that. "I don't lie, and when I make a plan, I stick to it."

"Then you've got nothing to worry about, Bill."

He knew that some people built their lives around trying to emulate their parents, but Bill had built his around trying to be as different from his father as possible. Carter Hastings III had been a man with no direction. So Bill had done his best to always have a plan, then stick to it. To be a man like his Uncle Jack, someone who kept his promises.

He liked his moral code.

But now, for the first time, he felt as if it

were biting him in the butt.

The next morning, Dori's phone rang, and out of some Pavlovian sort of drive, she picked it up without thinking.

"When are you bringing that Carter boy back?" Nana Vancy demanded in lieu of a standard salutation.

Dori wished she hadn't answered the phone.

She wished she'd gone outside to wait for Carter.

But she had picked it up, and she hadn't gone outside, and now she was stuck with her grandmother's interrogation.

"Nana, Carter's a friend. We've gone out a few times."

Okay, so saying they'd gone out went beyond exaggeration, but Dori didn't think it quite qualified as a lie.

They'd met at the Hazard Hills house, then at her house, they had gone out to lunch, and then yesterday they'd gone to see her grandparents. Three times was a few. Barely. One less and it would only have been a couple, and that didn't sound nearly as impressive. But *a few* . . . well, that was a dating number that had potential, at least in her grandmother's eyes.

"Well, we'd like to see him again soon,"

Nana Vancy continued.

Dori glanced out the front window, hoping beyond hope that Carter and his Civic would be outside. She sighed when she saw her empty driveway. "What you mean, Nana, is that you'd like to see him again soon because you're hoping I'll marry him and break your curse. Nana Vancy, I don't want you to pin too much hope on that. It's still way too early —"

"I know it's too early." Nana sounded affronted. "But that doesn't mean he's not the one, just that you don't know it yet. And that means you need to see him interact with your family, *lanyunoka*."

"I'll see about bringing him over again, but I won't promise."

Evidently that was all Nana needed. She switched topics. "So, you're taking him to your sister's today?"

"Yes," Dori admitted. She looked out the window again, praying the Civic would be there, but it wasn't.

"You call me when you get home from Vancy's and tell me how it went."

"Nana," Dori said with all the patience she could muster, "there's not going to be anything to tell. Carter's just going to take a look at the nursery and see if he has any suggestions, since Matt and Vancy can't seem to come to a compromise on their own."

"Call your grandmother, Dora Lee. After all, you promised."

"Promised what?" Dori often found conversing with her grandmother confusing. Nana Vancy never followed a straight conversational line; she weaved and bobbed in and out until Dori found herself totally lost. "I don't recall any promise about Carter."

"You promised you wouldn't care about your wedding. I need to know the boy better before I plan one."

"Nana, I really don't think you can call Carter a boy —"

"Anyone younger than me and male is a boy."

"And I'm not even sure you can call what Carter and I are doing dating. We've mainly talked business." She thought about last night on the beach and realized that hadn't been about business. She qualified, "We haven't shared our deepest secrets or dreams, haven't confessed our worst fears."

She realized that Carter *had* shared some of himself. *Stop and smell the roses* — the secret to his success, he'd said.

"You always did have unrealistic expectations," her grandmother groused.

"Nana, I'm going to be blunt here. I want

what you and Papa Bela have. What Mom and Dad have. What Vancy found with Matt, and what Noah found with Callie. If I can't have that, then I'll settle for being the family spinster who lavishes all her affection on her nieces and nephews. I'll buy a cat, maybe get Matt to help me start a garden, and, rather than worrying about dates, I'll just take care of that."

"Dori, *kedvenc*, there are many things in this life I don't understand. Mysteries I'll never solve. But one thing I know with absolute certainty is that you'll never be a spinster. It has nothing to do with second sight and everything to do with knowing what a special young woman you are. That Leo boy, he never saw that. You're better off without him."

"Nana, I just don't want you disappointed if things don't work out the way you'd like."

"I could never be disappointed in you, *lanyunoka*," her grandmother said softly.

Just as Dori started to melt, Nana Vancy added, in a tone reminiscent of a drill sergeant, "And call me when you get back from your sister's. Don't forget."

And with that, her grandmother hung up the phone.

"Family," Dori muttered under her breath. "You know what they say about people

91

who talk to themselves."

She turned and found Carter standing at her screen door. She glanced at her grandfather clock. "Hey, you're right on time."

"Too bad I wasn't early. Maybe I could have saved you from whichever family member called and left you muttering."

"My grandmother."

She could see from his expression that he got the picture. "Sorry. I know what that's like. My mom and aunt frequently tag-team my cousin and me. It can be brutal. What was she going on about?"

"Well, you see, my grandmother's already planning our wedding."

Carter choked on absolutely nothing. When his breathing evened out, he finally said, "Pardon?"

"My grandmother feels I'm to be the family's salvation. I need to find a man, marry him, and break the curse. And right now, you're the man in her crosshairs." She paused and added, "Sorry about that. We could skip out on Vancy's today. I can make some excuse."

"Is your grandmother going to be there?"

"No. But she'll hear about it. I can ask Matt and Vancy not to say anything, but she'll still hear."

"How?"

"Chris and Ricky are totally under her spell. They'll break and tell her anything she wants. She'll offer them a Nana Vancy story, and they'll cave like a house of cards. So, seriously, I wouldn't blame you if you backed out. My family — my grandmother in particular — can be daunting at best."

Bill knew he should take the out that Dori was offering him. It could be that easy.

He wouldn't have to go look at the nursery. He wouldn't have to fake his way through the design ideas CeCe had given him. He wouldn't get further enmeshed in this very odd, wedding-cursed family's business.

He could go home and get back into a nice pair of jeans and out of this *casual* outfit CeCe had stuffed him into. Another pair of pressed Dockers, this time with a button-down shirt and a tan T-shirt under it.

Yes, he should take the out Dori was offering him, go home, kick up his feet, and watch a game — whatever game was on. It wouldn't matter what sport. He'd take curling, or even rugby. Anything would be better than playing a part within a part.

Yes, he should say, *Okay, then, sorry it didn't work out.* Instead, he heard himself saying, "Dori, your grandmother doesn't scare me. We've got a nursery to go look at."

Something about Dori Salo touched him. He wasn't sure what it was. He wasn't sure why. But it did. As he'd told CeCe, he liked Dori. It was that plain and simple.

Unfortunately, his fabrication stood firmly between them. That and the fact that he was leaving town as soon as CeCe had the baby and was back on her feet.

So, rather than pursue his feelings, he'd simply continue to like Dori in a friendly way and not let it go deeper. "So, tell me more about your sister and brother-in-law on our way over there."

As they drove, Dori told him a long, romantic story about Vancy's being stood up at the altar and having the press hound her as they had a field day with the Salo Family Wedding Curse.

"I think I vaguely remember that," he said. "And I wasn't even in Erie. I was in Pittsburgh."

"Yeah, it was a national sensation. Vancy's ten minutes of fame."

"I thought it was fifteen minutes," he teased.

"Ah, she got the other five minutes in a supporting role when Noah's wedding plans fizzled."

He laughed. "Was the press bad then too?"

"Not as bad. But I'll confess, if I ever marry — and I have my doubts about that — the idea of the press having a field day with my wedding is less than appealing."

"I understand the press part, but what's this about your never marrying? A Mary Ann versus Ginger thing again?"

She shook her head. "Not exactly. Let's just say, once burned, twice shy. There was once a man I thought I'd spend the rest of my life with, but it turned out he wasn't who I thought he was. How can I trust my judgement?"

He glanced over at her, but she was staring out the car window as she continued. "How do you ever know if someone's who they say they are? How do you trust in that? I'm not sure. And until I know, I can't ever marry."

"Maybe when it's the right person, you just know."

"No. You *think* you know," she insisted. "There's no way to be sure."

"Maybe that's part of being in love. My mom always said there's no way to be absolutely positive about anything but death and taxes. Love is trusting that other person enough to go for it, regardless."

"I don't know if I can do that anymore, so

I'm pretty sure marriage isn't in the cards for me." Dori stopped and laughed. "I don't know how we got into such a deep discussion, but I hereby declare all serious talk done for the day. You and I have a nursery to look at."

"Dori, if you need to talk, I'm here." Well, he was here for now. He probably should say something about that. "I —"

Dori interrupted. "I don't want this to come out wrong, so let me just say thank you, Carter, but I think it would be better if we kept our future conversations about business."

She called him Carter, and it reminded him of how duplicitous he was being.

Maybe he should just confess the whole thing. But he'd promised CeCe.

He was saved from making a decision by Dori's saying, "We're here."

He pulled into the Front Street house's long drive.

"Just remember what I said," he urged her as they got out of the truck.

"I will," Dori promised as she started toward the house.

Dori wasn't sure why the discussion with Carter had shaken her up.

She glanced over her shoulder at the

preppy-looking man following her to Vancy's front door. Why did he affect her the way he did?

She didn't have time to puzzle over an answer, because the front door burst open, and Chris and Rick screamed in unison, "Aunt Dori!"

She wasn't their biological aunt, but, truth be told, she loved the boys as if she was, and by the way they jumped at her, hugging and tugging her into the house, she felt sure the feeling was reciprocal.

"Hi, sis," Vancy called as she waddled into the room.

Waddle was such a clichéd expression, but no other word better described Vancy's late-pregnancy gait. Wisely, Dori kept that thought to herself. "Hi. We're here, as promised."

"Hi, Carter. It's so very kind of you to come give us some ideas. There's nothing overly exciting about the room. And I'm not really someone who wants to invest a ton of money or time decorating a room that will be outgrown in short order. I might be a first-time mom, but having Chris and Rick has taught me that time around kids goes fast — very fast."

"Why don't we take a look at what you've got," he said, "and we'll see what we can figure out for you."

"That would be great." She led them through the living room.

Dori noticed Carter scanning the room and peeking through the doorway into the kitchen and dining area.

Vancy waddled down the hall, with Carter following her, and Dori, still entwined with little boys, followed at the rear.

"Here you go." Vancy threw open the door to what used to Matt's office.

"Where's the office now?" Dori asked. When her sister had first come to stay with Matt Wilde, this room had served as her bedroom. She'd thrown an air mattress onto the floor among Matt's office clutter and called it home.

Now the room was bare. All the furniture had been removed.

"Right now, Matt's office is in a corner of our room. Next summer, when things settle down, we're going to put on an addition. But for now, the bedroom office works." She turned to Carter. "Plain, isn't it?"

"Well, the window's marvelous." He walked over to it. "Nice view. You could put a small window seat there — something that can also be used to store toys or out-of-season clothes."

He continued. "And you're right, babies

grow up fast. So rather than going with a theme that will need to be changed in a year or so, what if you went with something that can grow with the baby?"

He did a complete circle of the room. "I couldn't help but notice, as we walked through your living room and I glanced into the kitchen, you seem to use a lot of natural colors."

"I'm not much of a pastels sort of woman. I like earth tones and order. No fussy doilies for me."

"Then why change that for this room?" Carter asked. "What if you kept the tan carpet and painted the walls a pale sage green. It's a gender-neutral color. You could use yellow and red as accent colors. It would be soothing, with bursts of color to keep it from being boring. That way you could incorporate Disney items or trucks or both, and as the baby grows and you get to know his or her personality, it won't be a big thing to modify the decor."

Dori noted that Carter looked uncomfortable, and she wondered what that was about.

"If you like, I can take the room's dimensions and sketch you something more detailed."

"No, no, that's perfect," Vancy assured

him. "I didn't expect you to do a whole design. I just wanted some ideas, and I like those. And really, a window seat is a great idea. Maybe I can convince Matt to do one in the boys' room as well."

"What are we convincing Matt to do?" Matt came into the room. "Hey, Dori. Carter, nice to see you again. We appreciate your coming out."

"My pleasure."

"Carter suggested a window seat," Vancy said. "Something with storage underneath. It should be fairly straightforward," she added hastily as she saw Matt's expression.

Dori didn't need to puzzle over Matt's lack of enthusiasm. He was great with the gardening stuff, but she knew that carpentry wasn't his forte.

"I could do it," Dori offered. "I've been trying to decide what to get the baby, and this would be perfect. But I wouldn't want to step on your toes if you really want to do it yourself, Matt."

Matt's expression of relief was evident as he laughed and said, "Well, Dori, you know how handy I am with lumber and a hammer, but I'll step aside because it's you."

"You are my favorite brother-in-law," she teased.

"And you're my favorite sister-in-law."

"Gack," Vancy said as she walked toward Carter and took his arm. "They're each other's *only* brother- or sister-in-law, so you could say they're each other's *least* favorite as well, but they never do. Let's get out of here and leave these two to their gross love fest."

She led Carter into the hall and steered him toward the kitchen. Dori and Matt followed on their heels.

Carter chuckled. "I thought it was rather cute."

"Cute in a gooey sort of way," Vancy said.

"I'm right here behind you," Dori said. "I can hear you."

"But I'm not talking to you," Vancy said. "I'm talking to Carter."

Chris and Rick ran up, and one pulled on each of Dori's hands. "Aunt Dori, will you build us a seat thingy like he" — Chris jerked a finger at Carter — "said? Like you're gonna build for the new baby?"

"I bet if you each drew me a new picture for my refrigerator, you could convince me."

"Come on, Chris," Rick shouted, "let's go start!" He turned to Dori. "We'll make 'em extra special."

"I'm sure you will."

The boys raced back down the hall to their room.

"Come on, Dori. I've got iced tea in the kitchen, and Matt got pizza."

"Oh, Matt, you didn't have to —" she started. But when her sister turned around, her eyes blazing with that particular pregnancy mania look, she amended herself. "Uh, if Vancy said so, I guess you did."

"She's been craving pizza lately," Matt said easily. "I mean, for breakfast, for lunch, and snacks. She'd probably have it for dinner, but the boys would want it too, and she's a stickler for good nutrition."

"You don't look as if you mind."

He shrugged. "I'm nuts about her. I'd eat pizza every day for a month if it would make her happy."

That's what Dori wanted — a man who would eat pizza for a month if it would make her happy.

They joined Vancy and Carter in the kitchen, and sat down to their impromptu lunch. Dori kept glancing at Carter. He was definitely the best-dressed one of them all. Matt was wearing jeans and an Everything Wilde — the name of his landscaping business — T-shirt. Vancy had on maternity shorts and a cute but plain white shirt.

Because Dori was learning that casual for Carter meant something entirely different than casual for the rest of them, she'd upgraded her look today to a polo shirt and a newer pair of jeans that still had that true-blue color. It hadn't helped. Next to him, she still felt dowdy.

"Dori, where are you?" Vancy asked, shaking Dori from her strange thoughts.

"Sorry. I was just thinking about the new site and everything I have to do tomorrow."

"You know that Papa Bela insists everyone takes the weekends off. He'd be annoyed if you were thinking about work. 'Mondays are for work. Weekends are for family,' " she quoted.

"You don't tell Papa Bela, and I won't tell about the time you and Noah broke Nana's —"

"Oh, that's so mean. And if Noah were here, he'd be protesting that he always gets sucked into our fights, even when he didn't do anything. Remember the time I decided to decorate your first hard hat?"

Dori laughed now, but at the time she'd been furious at Vancy. "All Noah did was try to break up the fight."

"And he got into trouble for 'fighting with girls.' Remember Dad? 'Boys do not hit girls — ever.' "

"Dad didn't seem to notice that Noah was the one who walked away with the black eye."

"They get like this," Matt said as an aside to Carter. "It's even worse when the whole family starts to reminisce."

Dori realized they were talking about things Carter Hastings couldn't possibly be interested in. "Sorry, Carter. We didn't mean to exclude you."

He smiled. "No worries. My cousin, CeCe, and I have all kinds of stories like that. For instance, the time she did my homework, and she was the one who got detention for cheating."

"Oh, she probably wanted to murder you," Vancy said. "I would have."

"Worse than murder. She got even. And CeCe seeking revenge is a scary thing."

"Do tell," Dori and Vancy said in unison.

Carter shook his head. "No way am I giving you two any ammunition."

"Thanks," Matt said. "I find it best not to give any of the Salos ideas. They have more than enough of their own. And I'll bet theirs rival your cousin's."

Carter eyed them both. Dori felt as if his gaze lingered on her longer than her sister, but that might have just been her imagination . . . or wishful thinking. She wasn't sure.

Carter grinned at Matt. "Yeah, those two look as if they could be trouble."

After they all had the pizza, Matt led Carter out to the backyard to show him his new truck.

"Well, they get along like old friends," Vancy said. She washed a cup and handed it to Dori to dry. "As a matter of fact, he fit in nicely with the whole family yesterday."

Dori wished her sister would stop studying her as if she were a bar exam. "Stop making those weird eyes at me, Vancy. It's not like that with Carter and me."

"It could be," she said slowly. "I saw how he looked at you."

Dori stopped drying the next glass. "Like a colleague? Or maybe he looked at me like a new friend?"

Friend. Yes, that was an apt description for what she and Carter were becoming. *Friends.*

"Well, I do think he likes you, but I think there's more to it than friendship." Vancy handed her a plate. "Dori likes Carter," she crooned in a singsong, playground sort of voice.

"This pregnancy is eating away at your brain cells," Dori assured her.

"I'm a lawyer. Remember? I'm trained to observe people, and I'm very good at what I do, if I do say so myself. There's more than friendship in Carter's brand of liking you."

"I think it's time I go collect my *friend*

and let him get back to his Sunday plans. He didn't sign on for all this Salo bonding time."

"Just keep it in mind. I think he likes you, and you like him."

"And I think this pregnancy is affecting your sanity." They walked out to the driveway, where the two men were deeply engaged in conversation.

"Hey," Dori called. "You two looked serious."

"We're thinking of going golfing on Saturday, and we were just discussing what course to play."

Ricky and Chris ran out of the house, pictures in hand. "Here, Aunt Dori. Do we get our window thingy now?"

She examined the pictures with all the seriousness she could muster. "They're beautiful, boys. You sure do."

"Speaking of next Saturday, Dori —" Vancy started.

Dori interrupted. She knew that look in her sister's eyes. "We were speaking of next Saturday?" she asked, playing dumb.

"The guys were talking about golfing on Saturday, so if you want to be literal, *they* were speaking of Saturday, and now I am. And I was going to ask you if you'd like to babysit Saturday night. Matt and I thought we'd try for one last pre-baby dinner out."

Dori couldn't stay annoyed with Vancy. She might be wrong about Carter, but she was pregnant and already raising two kids. She and Matt were going to be outnumbered. "You know I will."

"Can Carter come too, Aunt Dori?" Chris asked.

"Yeah!" Rick echoed.

"I don't think Mr. Hastings —" she started, trying to get Carter off the hook.

But at the very same time he said, "I'd love to, boys. As long as your aunt doesn't mind."

It wasn't just Carter's eyes on her. The boys were watching her, as were Vancy and Matt. So she simply nodded and said, "That would be nice."

And she wondered why her heart did a little leap at the thought that she'd be seeing Carter Hastings on a Saturday night.

She refused to comment on Vancy's softly humming the tune she'd used when she sang "Dori likes Carter."

She did like Carter, but not in the way Vancy was implying. At least she didn't want to like him in the way Vancy was implying.

If ever there was a man who was her polar opposite, it was Carter Hastings IV, the dressed-to-the-nines, hybrid-driving interior designer.

CHAPTER FIVE

Matt's golf game was far better than Bill's.

Matt ended up on par for the course.

Bill was over par. So far over he'd eventually given up keeping track of his score.

"That was just embarrassing," he said as he stuffed his clubs into his car.

Matt laughed. "I won't tell if you don't."

"Who would I tell?"

Matt smacked his back. "We should do this again. Maybe next time Noah will join us. Papa Bela isn't a golfer, but Dad is. That is, if you wouldn't mind."

"Why would I mind?"

Matt sighed. "Listen, you've been the buzz of the family all week. I thought I knew what I was getting into when I married Vancy. I mean, I thought I had an inkling of what a tight family the Salos were. I didn't even come close to imagining the reality of it."

"Oh?" Bill had spent an abnormal amount

of his week thinking about Dori Salo. Dreaming about Dori Salo. Wanting to phone Dori Salo. He'd refrained, knowing he'd be babysitting with her tonight, but it was a close call. And today he'd take whatever scraps of information Matt would throw his way about Dori or her family.

"I come from a sort of dysfunctional family," Matt said. "I'm rebuilding a relationship with my own father and stepmother. And my brother . . . well, he's trying, and we'll see where it goes. But the Salos? They live in one another's back pockets and like it that way. For instance, Vancy never intended to be a part of the family business, she resisted, but here she is, working for them now. Not because they pressured her or anything, but because ultimately that's where she wanted to be, where she belonged. Even me. I'm not a Salo by birth, but I'm doing most of the landscaping for Salo projects. Autonomous, but still a part of things."

"I'm not sure I see what you're getting at," Bill said.

"Carter, what I'm getting at is, the whole family is abuzz about you and Dori, trying to decide if this is just business, if it's a friendship . . . or if it's maybe something more. They're trying to give you some space. You got the entire week off — well, the weekdays — but I just want you to understand, that won't last. I don't think whatever you and Dori are developing is just a business thing. It might have started that way, but it's more. How much?" He shrugged. "I'm a guy — I'm not even trying to guess. But the women of this family won't hesitate guessing — and quizzing you for whatever info they can glean."

After they got into the car, Bill asked, "So what are you suggesting I do?"

"Figure it out. If you want more than just a friendship with Dori, be sure you can deal with her family. They're wonderful — don't get me wrong — but they're a big part of her life. Not everyone can handle that. I just figured you should know that coming in."

Bill wasn't sure what to say to that. "I appreciate it, and I do like Dori, but it won't be . . . it can't be anything more than a friendship."

"You already have a wife?" Matt teased.

When Bill didn't answer right away, Matt turned and glared at him. "You don't, do you?"

"No. No wife — now or ever. But I do have plans, and they don't include — can't include — a significant other. Especially not one that close to her family. I'll be leaving town soon."

Bill did have plans. He'd worked hard to save the money to go out on his own. Erie, Pennsylvania, was nice, but he wanted to head west. A friend had said the housing market out there was booming . . . that's what he wanted.

Yes, Erie was nice, but he wasn't staying.

He'd made a plan, and he was sticking to it. He wasn't someone to be swayed off course.

"Then make sure that Dori knows that, because . . . Ah, hell. There's no way to maintain my manly dignity and say this. I saw how she looked at you. Just make sure she knows that you two are only friends. I don't want her to end up hurt." He paused. "I like you, and I'd hate to have to make you regret it."

"Matt, I have to say, you're definitely a Salo now."

He grinned. "I know. It's great, isn't it?"

Despite the fact that he'd just been warned, Bill laughed. "Yes, it's great. Dori's lucky to have so many people who care about her."

"Uh, just don't tell her I was assigned the job of playing family enforcer. Dori wouldn't appreciate it, and I don't want to be on her bad side. I've heard stories about her ideas of revenge, and they're not pleasant."

"It's between you and me."

"Good. Now, about another golf game?"

They drove the rest of the way back to Matt's, and after a quick good-bye Bill headed home. He spent the rest of the day reflecting on Matt's words as he waited for his babysitting date with Dori.

"Earth calling Bill," CeCe said.

He forced himself to stop obsessing about Dori Salo and pay attention to his cousin. "Sorry. You were saying?"

"The doctor said it's not long now, so Mom's coming out next week. If you can wrap up the Salo deal, I should be able to take over in just a few weeks. You'll be free to go."

He should be thrilled.

He should be grinning from ear to ear at the thought of leaving town, guilt-free.

He should already be packing.

Instead, all he felt was a stab of regret that whatever spark it was he he had with Dori Salo would never have a chance to ignite.

"Bill?"

He gave himself a mental shake. "Sorry. That's great news."

"You're sure you're all right?"

"Positive." He glanced at his watch. "I'd better head out for my babysitting gig. You're sure you'll be okay?"

"I'll be fine," she assured him.

"You'll call if you need anything?"

"You've already fed and watered me. I'm fine. I'm just going to finish off this sketch." When he waited without saying anything, she quickly added, "But I'll call if I need anything."

He leaned down and kissed his cousin's forehead. "You know, our family might not be as big as the Salos, but it's every bit as important to me."

"Oh, Bill, that was uncharacteristically mushy for you."

He laughed even as he grimaced for comic effect. "Yeah, I'm pretty sure I strained something."

CeCe laughed. "Go. Have a good time."

"I will." He started out of the room.

"Hey, Bill?" CeCe called.

He turned around. His cousin looked more fair-complexioned than usual, but there was a radiance there. Despite being on her own, she loved this baby, and it already showed.

"Bill? Earth calling Bill."

He gave himself a mental shake. He had no idea why he was in such a touchy-feely mood tonight. "Yeah?"

"Be careful," CeCe warned.

"I don't —"

"I know you've only just met Dora Salo, only spent a handful of times with her, but there's something there. It's in your step, in your eyes, whenever you talk about her. And it's especially there tonight, when you're leaving here to go meet her. So, I'm just saying, be careful."

"You don't have to worry about the job . . ." he started. He let the sentence fade away as CeCe shot him a look of disgust.

"As much as I want this job" — CeCe had gone all stiff and formal — "you matter more to me than it does, more than even the business does. You should know that by now."

He'd hurt her feelings. He could see that. "Sorry."

"You should be," she huffed. "Now go. Wait. Turn around and let me have a look."

He was going to protest, but CeCe had that look in her eye, and he knew it was useless. He glanced down at the polo shirt and pressed khakis that were what CeCe felt were the most casual clothes *Carter* would wear.

"That's perfect. You look great."

Feeling anything but great, he headed out

to meet Dori at her sister's.

The excitement Dori had felt when she realized she'd be seeing Carter on Saturday night hadn't dimmed.

She'd forced herself to dress casually. An old softball T-shirt, mesh shorts, and sneakers. She wanted an outfit that said, *I didn't dress up for you.* And that's just what this one said — not with a whisper but a shout.

But despite her more-than-casual exterior, her interior was bubbling over with enthusiasm.

"Aunt Dori, Aunt Dori, come on!" Chris called from outside in the yard.

Dori forced herself to put away all thoughts of Carter and concentrate on the boys.

She lugged a heavy bucket to the window.

She slid the screen up and out of the way, then called, "Boys, what are you doing out there?"

Ricky and Chris both looked up. "You promised us a water fight," they said almost in unison.

"Did I?" she asked, feigning confusion.

"Come on, Aunt Dori," Rick said. "We filled our water guns."

"Last time you both ambushed me and got me when I least expected it."

"That's part of the fun with water fights — surprises," Chris informed her.

"Is it?"

Two dark-haired heads bobbled yes.

"Well, then . . ." She picked up one of the water balloons she'd loaded into the bucket and lobbed it out the window. It exploded at the boys' feet. "Surprise."

In quick succession she threw the rest, then surveyed the soaked twins. "Wow, you're right — that is the fun of water fights."

"Aunt Dori!" Ricky yelled.

"Yes, sweetie?"

"We're coming to get you."

"Sorry, boys. Your Aunt Vancy would have a fit if you traipsed through the house dripping all over her floor. But don't worry. I'll come out to you."

The boys yelled with glee and ran toward the clubhouse she had built them in the backyard.

Dori closed the screen and took the bucket downstairs with her. She deposited it in the kitchen, checked that her two water guns were secure in her waistband, grabbed her supersoaker rifle, and headed out the front door rather than the back. She was going to try for another sneak attack.

"Dori?" Carter was just getting out of his car.

"Shh!" She glanced around the perimeter of the front yard, hoping that the boys were still in the back waiting for her.

"What's going on?" he asked.

"A sneak attack. Can you handle yourself in battle?" She handed him one of her water pistols.

He grinned as he took it. "I think I can manage."

"Then follow me."

Dori crept along the side of the house. "They're in their treehouse, waiting for me. They don't know you're here yet. You sneak around the trees, and I'll walk into their ambush."

"You're the bait?" Carter asked.

"Yes." She nodded. "And you're the surprise attack."

"You're a wicked woman, Dori Salo."

"They ambushed me last time, and I'm all about getting even."

He laughed. "Be careful out there."

"You too."

She walked through the backyard, giving them a wide-open shot. "Oh, boys."

Twin heads popped out of the clubhouse window. "We've got you, Aunt Dori. Freeze."

Chris aimed a water gun, but Ricky held a plastic bucket likely filled with water.

At least Dori hoped it was water. With the twins, there were no guarantees. "Boys, you wouldn't."

"Oh, yeah, we would," Ricky cackled.

"Yeah," Chris agreed.

"Well, I guess I'm done for. I mean, what can I do? You have me covered." She dropped her water pistol to the ground and held up her hands in a sign of surrender.

She saw Carter climbing the ladder. He was quiet, like a cat.

"I mean," she said, eager to keep the boys talking so they wouldn't notice any noise Carter made as he climbed the ladder, "you two have *sooo* outsmarted me. I'm just a helpless girl. I can't beat you two."

The boys chortled with glee. Chris waved the water gun. "Come closer."

"All right. Anything you boys say." She took two very slow steps and saw Carter's feet disappear into the treehouse.

"Ah!" the boys cried.

Dori leaned down, grabbed her water gun, and started running toward them, ready to lend a hand, when Rick, in a heroic, last-ditch effort at revenge, threw the contents of the bucket at her.

She didn't have time to dodge the liquid

hurtling in an arc toward her.

Splat!

The boys continued to scream, and, despite the fact that she was drenched, Dori hurried to help Carter in the water battle to end all water battles.

Ten minutes later, all the guns were out of water. All water balloons and buckets were used up.

All that was left to bear witness to the great, almost epic, battle was the four of them, drenched.

Dori didn't even want to think about what she looked like. All she could do was stare at Carter. His once-pressed khakis were miserably sodden, and his equally neat polo shirt was stretched out from the weight of the water. And his shoes . . .

"Oh, man, Carter, I never even thought . . ." she said, wondering how on earth to make it up to him. "Your clothes are wet, but they'll probably survive. But your shoes. Oh, man, Carter, we've totally ruined another pair of your shoes. Callie's sister, Julianna, could probably tell us the make and model —" She realized what she'd said. "That's cars, not shoes, but you know what I mean. She'd be able to identify the designer, but I can't. I can, however, tell that those shoes were expensive, and now they're ruined."

She remembered the classy loafers he'd worn the first day she met him on the job site. "You've ruined two pairs of designer shoes because of me."

"Are we in trouble?" Chris asked.

"We're sorry, Carter," Ricky added.

"Hey, hey, all three of you, cut that out. They're only shoes. And if I'd been thinking, I'd have worn something more conducive to playing. So if a ruined pair of shoes is anyone's fault, it's mine."

"But they were expensive," Dori insisted.

"Nothing's worth more than watching you guys have fun. But, Dori, I think you should stop apologizing now, because you're spoiling the boys' fun."

She glanced at the twins, who wore identical expressions. They looked as if they were on the verge of tears.

"Carter's right. They're only shoes." She tried to infuse a chipperness into her voice that she didn't really feel. "So, how about we all go get changed, and then I'll treat you to ice cream?"

That was all the boys needed to hear. They scrambled down the ladder, across the backyard, and into the house.

"Speaking of changing, did you happen to bring other clothes?" Dori asked hopefully.

For a moment Carter hesitated, but then he nodded. "I have some old work clothes in the trunk of the car. I'll go get them."

Dori almost laughed as they descended the ladder, wondering what Carter's idea of work clothes would be. Designer boots? Name-brand sneakers and pressed jeans?

She smiled at the mental picture.

Whatever it was, he'd look cute in them.

He brought a small duffle bag with him when he came back to the house.

"You take the bathroom," Dori instructed him. "I'm going to use Vancy's room and borrow something of hers."

She kicked off her soaked sneakers and left them on the porch, then went into the house and to her sister's room. She dug through Vancy's drawers and found a pair of shorts and a T-shirt.

Barefoot, she stepped out into the hall, carrying her wet clothes, and found Carter coming out of the bathroom. "Hi," she said weakly.

He looked totally different.

Carter Hastings IV was a nice-looking man, but he'd been way too prissy for her.

This man, this Carter, looked like just one of the guys. His jeans were worn to that pale blue, almost white color. She knew if she touched them, they'd be soft from years of wear. Just thinking about touching them set her heart racing.

He had on a equally faded T-shirt that hugged his body in a way no pleated dress shirt or polo shirt could. It emphasized that he either worked out on a semiregular basis or had been gifted with good genes.

Very good genes.

"Dori?" he asked. "You okay?"

She tried to swallow but found her mouth too dry to manage it, so she just nodded. She forced herself to collect her wits and said, "My clothes are soaked. I was going to toss them over the shower rod."

"That's what I did too."

She went into the bathroom and found his clothes draped over the rod. She did the same and tried not to notice how sweet their clothes looked hanging together.

"Dori?"

She turned and found Carter giving her an odd look. "Sorry, did you say something?" she asked.

"I said, let's go get that ice cream."

"My shoes are wet."

"I'll drive and bring your ice cream to the car."

She nodded, trying to ignore the fact that Carter had ditched his ruined designer shoes in favor of a scuffed pair of sneakers.

She really liked the look of this Carter. And she'd liked him even when he was the fussy Carter.

He made her laugh.

He didn't mind goofing around with the kids.

He was a man who recognized that kids were more important than shoes.

He was . . . nice.

"Let's go," she said. She wasn't going to think about how cute Carter was. How nice he was. How real he seemed.

They were here to babysit the kids.

Nothing more.

Dori had been giving Bill odd looks all night. Even when he didn't catch her at it — and he did catch her at it a lot — he could feel those eyes boring holes into him.

It seemed to start around the time they'd gone for ice cream.

He couldn't decide what it meant.

All he knew was that as she gave him her weird looks, he was pretty sure he was giving her ones as well. Because all he could think of was how nice it would be to kiss her. And how cute her pink toenails were.

Yes, practical, work-clothes-wearing Dori had fancy-looking pink polish on her toes.

It was sexy as all get out.

Very sexy.

He wanted to tell her as much, but all he could hear was Matt and CeCe's warnings in his ear.

They'd gotten the boys to bed . . . finally. Then they had gone outside and were sitting on Matt and Vancy's porch swing.

For long minutes they sat in silence, enjoying the night. Over the bluff, Bill could make out dots of light on the dark lake, boats out in the bay. To the right, the dock was lit up, the Bicentennial Tower standing brightly at its tip.

At first the silence was comfortable, as if he and Dori had been friends for years, long enough to not require constant chatter.

But as the minutes grew longer, and the only sound came from crickets chirping in the grass, the silence grew heavy and uncomfortable.

It felt as if the weight of his deception was bearing down on Bill, making it hard to breathe. "Dori?"

"Hmm?"

"I've got a couple things I need to tell you." A sense of relief flooded over him as he said the words. But just as quickly, he knew he couldn't break CeCe's confidence. He'd simply have to settle for telling Dori what he could.

"Okay," she said.

"First, I want you to know that, as soon as I'm able, I'm planning to move out west."

"Why?"

"There's a lot of opportunities for a solo" — he almost said architect and quickly substituted — "designer."

"Oh." She paused. "Was that all?"

"No. I wanted you to know that up front because right now, I really want to kiss you, but I wanted you to know that, while I'm attracted to you, I will be leaving town eventually. I wouldn't want to hurt you or have you feel I led you on. I will be leaving town."

"What about Hastings Designs and your cousin?"

"My cousin understands why I'm leaving. And I needed you to understand I was going, because, like I said, I want to kiss you." He gently placed a finger under her chin and tilted her head toward him. "I would never want to hurt you, Dori."

"Carter, I'm not looking for what the rest of my family has. I'm not searching for a long-term commitment. So, to be honest, the fact that you're leaving, that we both know whatever we become has an expiration date, is good."

She leaned in and kissed him. It was a

featherlight kiss that served as an introduction. She pulled back and looked at him shyly.

"I do understand, Carter."

Bill.

He wanted to tell her to call him Bill. But he couldn't until CeCe released him from his promise. Thinking about how he'd met Dori, he wanted to make sure she understood how things stood regarding more than just his impending departure.

"This has nothing to do with Hastings Designs."

She nodded. "I never thought it did. And, for the record, I'd already decided to use Hastings."

He kissed her this time. Her arms wrapped around his neck, holding him close.

"Want to spend the day together tomorrow?" Bill wanted — no, needed — to be with her as much as he could for as long as he could.

She smiled. "I'd like that."

"Maybe we could go fishing?"

Dori moved her head from his shoulder and looked up at him. "Really? Fishing, Carter?"

"You think I can't fish?"

"It's just that . . . well, you don't dress like a fisherman."

He laughed. "No, I don't suppose the clothes you've seen me in would qualify. But I'll pick you up tomorrow, and you'll see."

"I can't wait." She laid her head back on his chest.

Bill could have held her forever, but a small voice said, "Aunt Dori, there's a monster under the bed!"

Dori smiled at him. "Sorry." Then she hurried off without waiting for his response.

"Me too," Bill whispered.

Not sorry he'd kissed her, but sorry he'd ever allowed CeCe to talk him into this wacko scheme.

CHAPTER SIX

"Bill, really, you can't go out like that," CeCe complained the next morning as she eyed his outfit.

His well-worn cargo pants, *I'd Rather Be Fishing* T-shirt, and his fishing hat with all the hooks and lures on it was not what CeCe considered a fashion statement. He'd known that as he put on the clothes.

"CeCe, no matter how 'metrosexual' a guy is, he can't wear designer labels fishing."

"But if you'd warned me, I could have found something better than that. At least leave the hat."

"I'm not the Ken in your Barbie collection, CeCe. When I've been representing your company, I've humored you. But this is fishing, and I swear, any one of your outfits would scare any reputable fish away."

"But what will Dora think?" she practically whined.

"Dori will think I'm a man who knows

how to dress for any occasion. Now, do you need anything before I go?"

"No, I'm fine."

He didn't say anything, just raised an eyebrow.

"Okay, maybe you could get me something to drink first. Then, I swear, I'll stay put."

He didn't just get her a glass of juice; he stuck the entire container into a bowl of ice and brought it in. "There. No excuse to get up at all."

"Except to use the bathroom if I drink all that." She laughed. "Really, you've thought of everything. I'm fine. My friend Muna's dropping by with lunch, so it's all good. Go."

"Then I'm off."

"Hey, Bill," she called.

He turned around at the doorway. "You need something else after all?"

"I just need you to be careful. You've been spending a lot more time with Dora Salo than a business deal requires."

"Fishing has nothing to do with business."

"That's what I'm afraid of. I don't want to see you hurt. Her either, for that matter."

"I told her last night that I was leaving town as soon as I'm able. She knows this isn't the real-deal, rest-of-our-lifetime sort of thing. It's just two people who like each other spending time with each other."

"If you say so." She didn't look convinced.

"I do. Now, relax. I'll be back in time to get you dinner."

"Feed the fat lady. Nice, Bill."

"Not fat, just pregnant." He paused and added, "Very, very pregnant."

"Go before this very, very pregnant lady forgets the whole bed-rest thing and reminds you who frequently won our childhood wrestling matches."

He went, but CeCe's warning dimmed some of his excitement.

Dori had offered to drive, and when he checked out the window and saw her pull up in front of the house, he saw why. There was a small boat being towed by her truck.

He opened the door and walked outside, just as she got out of the truck and started toward the house. "Nice boat," he called.

She stopped and grinned. "Noah called it *The Wreck* when I bought it, and that's what I christened it when I got it lake-worthy."

It was a small, maybe fifteen-foot, motorboat. Despite its lack of size, it practically shimmered, it was so well polished. *The Wreck* was neatly stenciled at the front.

"It's not a wreck now," he said.

"That, my friend, is an entire winter's worth of work. I'd probably have gotten off cheaper building my own or buying new."

"But you enjoyed the challenge."

She grinned. "You're right. I did."

"So, are you going to share your best fishing spot with me?"

"It's a secret spot, but, yes, I'll share. But you've got to pinky-swear never to tell."

"When I make a promise, I don't break it. Ever." He realized that his serious tone wasn't warranted by Dori's teasing request, so he smiled and held a pinky aloft. "I pinky-swear I'll never tell."

She wrapped her pinky around his, and they took off for the lake.

Dori couldn't get over how different Carter looked because of a simple change of clothes. He had on another well-worn pair of jeans, a T-shirt, and a light denim shirt over that. But the kicker was the floppy hat with a fishing license pinned to it, along with an array of hooks and lures.

It was a hat that had been out on a lake more than once. It spoke of comfort, of someone who liked being outdoors.

And an outdoors man was the last thing she'd have pegged Carter Hastings IV as.

He was a man of contradictions, and she didn't quite know what to make of that.

Last night he'd kissed her — after making

sure she knew he was leaving.

An honest man.

She knew that her grandfather, father, and brother were honest men. Matt too. But still, she thought men like Carter were rare.

"I don't think your secret spot is working," Carter said. They were the first words either of them had spoken for almost an hour. They'd spent the afternoon on the boat, even eating the lunch Dori had packed.

The silence had been comfortable as the boat floated in the peninsula's lagoon.

"You know how it is with fishing — some days you hit it, and some days you don't. I think we can head in and chalk up today to one that you don't."

Carter glanced at his watch. "I have to get home by dinnertime anyway."

Dori felt a flash of disappointment. She'd thought she and Carter would spend the whole day together. She gave herself a stern mental shake. Of course Carter had other things to do. "Sure, we'll head in."

She turned around and started the motor, angling the boat toward shore.

"Dori, maybe after I see that my cousin's fed, we could get together for dinner ourselves — unless you have a family thing."

"Even if I had a family thing, you'd be

133

invited. But, no, we don't have anything planned for this weekend."

"Then dinner later?"

"You're sure?"

"Of course, I'm sure, or I wouldn't have asked."

"Then, yes."

When they got out, Dori backed the boat's trailer down the ramp, and Carter was left to load the boat on. She threw the truck into park and, out of the corner of her eye, saw Carter give a tug. But he pulled himself off balance and into the water.

Splash!

"Carter?" Dori called as she got out of the truck's cab.

He was standing, dripping water, as she got around to the back.

"Why is it that every time I'm around you, I find myself soaked?"

"Hey, at least it wasn't a fall into a muddy hole this time."

"So, what you're saying is, there's always a bright side?"

"Well, not always, but frequently."

He laughed. "Okay, let's get this loaded, then figure out how I'm getting home without soaking the inside of your truck."

They made short order of it, and Carter ended up sitting on an old blanket she kept stuffed behind the truck's seats.

He didn't invite her into the house but said, "I'll get cleaned up, take care of a couple things, and shoot over to your place to pick you up."

"Where are we going?"

"Let's do a traditional movie and dinner, if that's all right."

"As in a traditional date?" she asked.

"That's what I'd like, but if you'd rather —"

"Yes," she said, cutting off his sentence.

He grinned. "I'll be there soon."

Dori was still smiling when he got to her place two hours later and knocked on her door.

He was wearing another version of "casual" clothes.

"You're ready," he said, sounding surprised.

"Yes. But come in. I want to take care of something before we go."

"Yes?"

She handed him a file. "As I said yesterday, the job's officially yours. I don't want you to think it's because of this. We've had friendly outings, but this is the first one we've called a date, and I wanted to be sure you didn't think . . ." She hesitated. "Well,

Hastings Designs got the job on its own merit. My decision wasn't influenced by the fact that I like you or that we're dating, okay?"

He nodded. "Okay. CeCe will be thrilled."

"So now, let's go on a date. A regular, movie-and-dinner first official date."

"As long as we're being up front, I just want to remind you that I am leaving town soon."

"I didn't forget." But the thought of Carter's leaving left her feeling a profound sense of . . . sadness? No, it was worse than that.

Dori didn't explore it. As a matter of fact, she didn't plan to think about it at all. She was going to concentrate on the here and now and enjoy the evening with Carter Hastings IV.

She was going to enjoy their time together for however long they had.

CHAPTER SEVEN

Three weeks.

Dori smiled to herself at the thought.

It had been three amazing weeks with Carter.

They were sitting in the middle of her Hazard Hills living room. Or, rather, the space that would one day be the living room.

Carter had the final design plans laid out in front of her — sketches and colors and fabric swatches.

"I like it."

"Then we have the okay?"

She nodded.

Carter pushed away the samples and sketches and leaned forward, so close, their lips were almost touching. "I'm glad that's over. I have other things on my mind."

"Oh? Do tell."

"Well, first we're going to —"

Carter's cell phone interrupted him. "Sorry," he said as he pulled it out of his pocket and glanced at the caller ID. "I've got to take this."

A smile crept over his face as he answered whatever the caller was saying with a series of "okays". He clicked the phone shut and stood. "I've got to go. I'll make it up to you."

As she stood, he gathered up all his things and, without ceremony, dumped them into his crisply new-looking briefcase. "I'll call you tomorrow." He gave her a brisk kiss on the cheek and bolted out of the partially finished house.

"Good-bye to you too," she muttered.

What now? She'd planned on spending her evening with Carter, but now that he was gone . . .

Her cell phone rang. She smiled. He was probably calling to talk. "Hello?"

"Dori, it's me." It took her a minute to realize the *me* in question was Vancy, because her sister didn't sound like herself. "It's time."

"Time for what?"

"The baby. It's time. Can you meet me at the hospital?"

Dori's speed as she left the house rivaled Carter's. Her sister was going to have a baby. Everything else faded away in the face of that fact.

138

■ ■ ■ ■

Knowing that CeCe's pregnancy had been a difficult one, Bill was nervous about the actual delivery.

He'd seen flashes of videotaped births as he flipped through the Discovery Channel. He always flipped fast because he found the entire process disturbing.

Very disturbing.

CeCe had called her mom and his mom, and the cavalry was coming, but he had to hold down the fort until they arrived.

"Bill, seriously, stop pacing." Propped in the hospital bed, grinning with excitement, CeCe didn't look nearly as nervous as he felt. "I'm going to have a baby. My baby. Soon. But your pacing's making me seasick, and that takes some of the fun out of it."

"How long do you think it will take them?" he asked again.

"It's about five hours from Harrisburg. And since we called almost that long ago, I'd say it will take them less than that five hours now, and hopefully they'll be here soon."

"Yes. You're right." He stopped pacing long enough to study her intently. "You don't look like you're ready to pop the baby out."

"I'm not. Not yet."

"Good. Keep it that way — at least until they arrive."

"I'll try." She patted the bed to indicate he should sit.

Bill went to her and sat down by her side. "I know this pregnancy has been hard on you, but, seriously, CeCe, you're about killing me."

"Sorry," she said with a laugh, which had been his intent.

"This is worse than the time you convinced me to go wall-climbing with you."

"How was I to know? I mean, think about all those movies where characters used tied-together sheets. No one ever fell down a cliff face on television."

"Well, in addition to having a whole team of prop people helping set things up, I think there's a very good chance they used better knots than you did."

"Hey, if you'd stuck with that Boy Scouts stuff, you'd have known a better way." She paused, their joking forgotten as another contraction hit.

"Breathe," Bill said — not that he had any idea what he was doing, but on TV that's what they always said to women having contractions.

"Seriously, seriously, CeCe" — he didn't want to ask, but he knew he had to — "is there anyone you want me to call?"

"I've already called my mom and yours, and you're here, so who's left to call? We're good."

He could tell by her stubborn expression that she knew what he'd meant, but since she was going to play dumb, he spelled it out. "By 'anyone,' I meant the baby's father."

"The baby doesn't have a father."

"CeCe. What happened? You still haven't told me."

"And I'm not going to. All you need to know is, this is my baby."

"Since the baby doesn't a father, he or she will just have to settle for an uncle . . . well, cousin. Second cousin?"

"Let's just stick with uncle," she said, laughing.

"Good. But what I was trying to say is, this baby has me."

CeCe's expression grew serious. "Bill, I know you'll love the baby, but you'll be in another state at the other end of the country. The rest of the family, such as it is, is out of town as well. This baby will have me. That's going to have to be enough."

Her words struck him. He'd be half a country away. The thought didn't sit well, but he didn't have time to ponder it. He held CeCe's hand as the doctor came in and gave her an epidural.

As much as he didn't like needles, this time it didn't even bother him, because the relief was almost instantaneous for CeCe, and for that he'd have taken the needle himself.

Twenty minutes later his mother and aunt came into the room. "Bill, honey," his mother said as she absently kissed his cheek, then hurried to join her sister at CeCe's side.

Bill left quietly, leaving CeCe in their care, and went to look for the waiting room, where all self-respecting uncles-to-be should wait.

A nurse directed him down the hall, but instead of finding a quiet, empty room, he found bedlam.

And this particular bedlam was the kind he was quickly becoming familiar with, since it was of the Salo variety. What were the odds, he wondered, of a Salo and a Hastings delivery on the exact same day?

"Carter!" Ricky and Chris called as they bounded over to him. "We're here to get us a brother!"

Dumbstruck, he asked simply, "What if it's a sister?" Then he felt bad, because the look on the twins' faces said they didn't believe there was even the remotest chance of that.

"Ah, Carter. What are you doing here?" Nana Vancy asked, echoing his own surprise.

"My cousin's having her baby." He looked at the assembled Salo clan but didn't spot the one face he wanted to see most. "Where's Dori?"

"She went in with her mother to be with Vancy. It seems our Matt is feeling a bit queasy about the whole thing."

"Oh." Bill didn't blame Matt in the least. Now that he'd been replaced, he realized how tight his own stomach felt.

"You just sit with us, and we'll wait together," Dori's grandmother instructed.

"Okay."

"I brought cookies," she added.

Even if his stomach wasn't in a state, Bill didn't stand a chance at beating the twins to the cookies. But Ricky and Chris brought one over to him before taking the whole plate into a corner and having at it.

People chattered around him. Papa Bela, Noah, Callie, Dori's dad, Nana Vancy — even the boys, once the cookies were finished off. But all he could do was think of

CeCe and worry about her.

He desperately wished his mother or aunt would come out of her room and fill him in. His uncle had gone to the hotel to wait, his aunt had said. Uncle John was very hospital-phobic. He said he'd rather wait to meet his grandchild when he or she came home.

People bustled around, talking and laughing, and somewhere along the line, time lost all meaning. There was no clock in the room, and Bill wasn't wearing a watch.

He sat quietly in the midst of the chaos. After a while Nana Vancy came and sat next to him. "You're close to this cousin?"

"We were raised like siblings. We lived right next door to each other and were both only children. The same age. I'm closer to her than most brothers are to their sisters." He thought of Noah and his sisters and amended the comment. "Like Noah is to Dori and Vancy. We've got a small family, but we're tight, like all of you."

"It doesn't matter how big or how small a family is. What matters is being there for one another. You might not be in the room, but your cousin knows you're here, just like our Vancy knows we're all here. That's what matters."

She let him be then, which was fine,

because with every passing minute, Bill grew more and more concerned. CeCe had been on bed rest because of complications. What if there were more to come?

What if something happened to the baby?

What if something happened to her?

Who would care for the baby?

He realized that her mother or his might want to, but they were both older. He and CeCe had been change-of-life babies for the sisters. They had them when they'd long since given up hope of having children. He couldn't imagine them keeping up with an infant's demands day after day.

But he could.

And he realized that not only could he, but he'd want to. He'd talk to CeCe. Maybe she'd allow him to be more than the baby's cousin-y sort of uncle. Maybe she'd let him be the baby's guardian.

He started rethinking leaving Erie, about moving out of state and never seeing CeCe's child except for holidays. He'd hate that.

Then he thought of Dori. If he left town, he'd be leaving her behind too.

He realized he didn't want that. Didn't want that at all.

Bill Hastings was a man who kept his word, who always laid out a plan, then stuck to it. But he wouldn't really be changing his plan so much if he stayed in Erie. He'd just be altering it. He could open his own architectural firm here. If the city was big enough for Hastings Designs, maybe it could handle Hastings Architectural.

Another thought occurred to him. Maybe it could handle Hastings Interior and Architectural Designs.

Would CeCe be willing to form a partnership?

With the money he'd saved to invest in a solo firm, they could afford to move from her cramped home office to a real office, something big enough for both of them.

He could stay in Erie, help CeCe with the baby.

He could stay in Erie and continue seeing Dori.

Then he realized that if he did that, he'd have to come clean with her.

It wasn't a huge deception, after all. He'd said he was working with CeCe, and if CeCe did agree to a partnership, what he'd told Dori would be more of an omen than a deception.

Of course, Dori would have to get used to the way he normally dressed, and she'd have to learn to call him Bill.

Maybe, eventually, they'd laugh about it?

As if on cue, Dori chose that moment to

walk into the room. Everyone grew silent, waiting.

"We have a girl!" she cried.

Smiles abounded among everyone but Chris and Rick. As Nana Vancy started to weep, one of the boys said, "Let's call her Yucky," while the other one said, "I don't want a sister."

"The doctor said if you hold on a while longer, everyone can go meet her before you go home."

Everyone bubbled over and moved toward the door, as if the closer they got, the faster they'd get to see Vancy and the baby.

No one else seemed to notice the twins' upset. "Hey, guys," Bill said, "she might be a sister, not a brother, but maybe you can teach her to be a tomboy. Look at your Aunt Dori. She does all the cool things any boy might do."

Chris and Rick said, "Yeah," in unison and looked decidedly happier.

Dori, however, was standing nearby. "I do cool things like a boy?"

"Yeah. You have water fights," Chris said.

"And build houses," Rick added.

"Hey, she even fishes," Bill said. "Maybe your sister will grow up to be just like your Aunt Dori."

"Yeah." Both boys, obviously pleased at

the thought, hurried toward Nana Vancy.

"Your cousin?" Dori guessed.

He nodded.

"How is she?"

"Still waiting." He looked at Dori and realized that, though CeCe and the baby were two big reasons he wanted to stay in Erie, Dori was an even bigger one. "Congrats, Aunt Dori."

"I don't think I've ever seen anyone as excited as Matt. He went from green to beaming in the blink of an eye."

"Are you going back in?" he asked.

"No, I'm going to give them some time to themselves before the whole crew goes in."

"I need to talk to you." He wanted very much to tell her everything, especially the part about staying in Erie and wanting to have more time with her.

Who was he kidding?

He didn't want to spend more time dating her or hanging out with her. He wanted more. Much more. A lifetime of more.

The thought surprised him.

A lifetime with Dori?

It had only been three weeks since they met. And rational thought would say that wasn't enough time. But, looking at her, standing there in hospital scrubs and practically glowing over her new niece, he knew that what they had, what it could grow into, was the stuff lifetimes together were built out of.

"Carter," Dori said, snapping her fingers in front of his eyes. "Hey, Carter, come out of the clouds."

He grinned hugely and knew it was a ridiculous expression, but, looking at her standing there, he just couldn't help it. "Sorry. What did you want?"

"I was asking what you wanted to talk about."

He took a deep breath and said, "There's been a misunderstanding. . . ." That was a cop-out. "More than that, you see, CeCe asked me —"

Chris and Rick ran over and interrupted. "Aunt Dori, Aunt Dori, tell us about our sister."

Dori took Chris onto her lap, and Bill followed suit and took Ricky onto his.

"Your sister is very beautiful. She's got dark hair —"

"Like us?"

Dori nodded. "Just like you both. Her eyes are blue, but most baby's are. That might change."

"Maybe she'll have brown eyes like us?" Chris asked.

"Maybe. She cried for a minute, but then

Matt handed her to Vancy, and she stopped. Vancy held her, and she looked around, checking everyone out. She was looking so hard that her eyes crossed like this." Dori crossed her eyes and puckered her lips, much to the boys' delight.

A nurse came to the door. "Dori, Vancy asked if you'd bring the boys in first."

Dori nodded. "Carter, we'll talk later, if that's okay."

They'd gone on three weeks with his deception. Another night wouldn't hurt. "It'll keep."

She kissed his cheek, then blushed as her family all crooned, "Oooh."

"Grow up, you guys," she said as she took each boy by the hand, then walked out the door.

Noah walked over to Bill. "So, you and my sister."

Bill eyed Dori's older brother, then nodded. "Yes. Dori and me."

"Matt says you're moving soon." The words came out as more of a challenge than an inquiry.

"Nothing's been decided for sure." Actually, it had been. Bill knew he wasn't going. But he was also sure the first person he discussed that decision with wouldn't be Dori's brother.

"Matt also said he warned you about hurting her."

"He did, not that he needed to. I care for Dori." The words felt like an understatement. He more than cared. He . . .

"Did he tell you about Leo?"

Noah's question derailed Bill's thoughts, and he shook his head.

Noah sat down next to him. "Carter, I should just keep quiet and mind my own business. That's what Callie would tell me. But right now she's distracted by all this baby business, so I'm going to do what I think is right. Dori will kill me if she knows I told you."

"But you're going to tell me anyway?"

Noah nodded. "Leo and Dori dated all through high school. They got engaged their senior year of college."

"Not another wedding casualty, courtesy of the Salo Family Wedding Curse?"

"It never got that far. Leo left."

"Left?" Bill echoed.

"He went off to grad school and told Dori that when he got done, they'd plan the wedding. Three weeks later, he called —"

"And broke up with her?"

"No. Told her he loved her and to start the plans for their wedding and their life together. She spent a year planning the wedding. She didn't care about the curse, didn't care about anything except one day being Jason Leonardo's wife."

Hearing about Dori and another man hurt more than it should, given the amount of time they'd known each other. Part of Bill didn't want to hear anything else; the other part felt he needed to know. That was the part that won out. "And?"

"Leo waited a year and a half to break up with her. He called her . . . after he married someone else."

"Oh." Bill hated this Leo and knew that Dori was lucky to find out sooner rather than later what a snake he was.

"I don't know if you were planning on trying for a long-distance relationship — to be honest, I don't know what you're planning at all, and I'm not asking. But I will say, it wasn't the fact that they broke up that destroyed Dori. They were young, and I don't know that anyone but Dori was completely surprised. No, what was so hard on her was that he'd lied to her and led her on. I think that's what hurt Dori the most."

"I told Dori I'd be moving," Bill pointed out.

"I know. Whatever you two decide, just be up front with her. And if you hurt her —" Noah took on a big-brother, protective demeanor.

"You and Matt? You're both warning me?"

"Me, Matt, and every other member of the Salo family. To be honest, I think the men are the least of your worries. Mom and Nana are sort of scary. And Vancy can sure hold her own. Dori hasn't been serious about anyone since Leo. But when she looks at you . . ." He shrugged. "I just don't want to see her hurt."

"Neither do I," Bill admitted. "I'll bear that in mind."

"Good."

"Bill?" his mother said from the doorway. He looked up, then noticed that Noah was giving him an odd look, a questioning look. He realized that his mother had called him Bill, not Carter, and rather than wait around for Noah's questions, he hurried to his mother. "CeCe?"

"It's a boy." She looked delighted. "He looks just like you did when you were born."

"Good. Then at least we know he'll be handsome," he teased.

His mother laughed, then took his arm and pulled him toward the door.

"It's a boy, and I've gotta go," Bill called to the Salos before he followed his mother out the door and down the hall.

He tried not to worry about the Salos as

he hurried down the hall next to his mom. "They're both fine?"

"Perfect." She grabbed his arm and brought him to a halt, then stood on tiptoe and kissed his cheek.

"What was that for?"

"I couldn't help but remember when you were born. Like I said, he looks just like you. That weird clump of hair in the middle of his head and the inquisitive expression. I swear, he's trying to figure out the whole world already."

"Bright boy."

"Just like his cousin."

"Uncle. CeCe and I decided we were closer than most siblings, much less cousins, so I'm going to be his uncle."

"He'll need one. Your Aunt May is so worried about CeCe doing this on her own. We're not that far from Erie, but far enough. When you move, she'll be here on her own with the baby." His mother's happy expression faded. "I remember what it was like when your father left. And you weren't an infant. You were five. It's so hard to raise a child on your own. I just don't think CeCe knows what she's in for."

"Maybe she won't have to do it alone. Things change, you know."

His mom gave him the look he remembered so well from when he was growing up. It was an expression that asked, *What's going on?*

Once it would have made him nervous, but now he laughed. "I'm not ready to talk about it, but I'm rethinking my plans."

"You never rethink plans," his mother pointed out. "I've never met anyone so focused on his goals."

"Times change. Things change. Even me. You're right. CeCe might not know it, but she needs family here."

His mother kissed him again. "You always were a good boy."

"That's not what you used to say," he reminded her as they started back down the hall.

"I just didn't want to give you a swelled head."

They stopped outside CeCe's door. "Hey, Mom. Do you ever hear from Dad?"

"I know John's talked to him a few times. But no, he doesn't call me."

"Oh."

"Bill, your father had problems. He still does. They had nothing to do with you or me. His leaving us was just a byproduct of those problems. It wasn't that he didn't love us. He just loved alcohol more."

"Yeah, I know. I just wondered. Dori's

155

sister and brother-in-law are raising his nephews. They've made me think about how lucky I was to have Uncle John in my life. And you, Aunt May, and CeCe too. It's not a big family, but it's a good one."

She kissed his cheek again. "Wondering about your father is natural. And if you ever want to talk, you know I'm here. But now, come meet the newest addition to the family."

The entered the room. CeCe was sitting up in the bed, looking tired but practically glowing with happiness. "You want to hold him?"

"I don't know . . ." he started, but CeCe was already thrusting the baby in his direction, and before he knew it, Bill was indeed holding the tiny bundle.

In his opinion, the baby resembled Yoda. He wasn't a plump Gerber baby, but rather a skinny little bundle of humanity. His hair was so blond, what little of it there was was practically invisible.

Maybe Yoda crossed with Bruce Willis.

Then he blinked his dark blue eyes at Bill. "He's looking at me."

It was an intent look that belonged to someone much older than the half hour or so the baby was. He studied Bill as if he wasn't quite sure about him.

"He likes you," CeCe said. "Bill, I'd like you to meet Cameron William Hastings. I thought we'd call him Cam. Cam, meet your godfather, Uncle Bill."

"You gave him my name?"

"Bill, if he grows up to be half the man you are, I'll count myself lucky." CeCe sniffled. The sniffle led to out-and-out tears.

"CeCe . . ."

"Don't mind me. I'm just sort of a hormonal wreck."

Bill must have still looked concerned, because his mom said, "May, remember after I came home with Bill? We stood there, each holding a baby, and we just burst into tears."

His aunt May laughed. "We were quite the pair."

"What do you mean, *were?*" his mom asked, then promptly broke into tears.

"Oh, June."

Suddenly Bill found himself surrounded by three crying women. And they weren't the kind of tears a man could comfort or jolly them out of. He was wise enough to realize that all he could do was weather the storm.

"It's every man's nightmare," he whispered to Cam.

He was pretty sure the baby agreed.

After his mom and aunt went down to the cafeteria for coffee, Bill was left alone with CeCe, who had retrieved the baby.

"I'm going to let you get some sleep," he said. "You don't look as if you can keep your eyes open much longer."

"I am tired."

"In a couple of days, I'd like to talk to you." He'd made up his mind and had an addition to his plan, but it could wait until CeCe was back on her feet.

CeCe didn't look tired any longer as she asked, "About?"

"A business proposition."

"Don't leave me on pins and needles, Bill. What business proposition? Something to do with the Salos? Is there a problem with the designs?"

"Nothing like that. I was wondering if you'd be interested in taking on a partner. Don't answer now," he added. "It's just that, well, given that I'm about to become Cam's godfather, as well as his cousin-y sort of uncle, and given the fact that we've worked together well, I thought, rather than investing my money in a business out west, I should maybe stay here, close to our family . . . close to you and Cam."

CeCe started to cry again.

"Oh, gee, CeCe, it was just an idea. I

mean —"

"Oh, Bill!" she wailed, which woke the baby with a start and set him to wailing as well. "I'm not crying because you've upset me, but because I'm so happy," she said as she bumped the baby up and down against her shoulder.

For the life of him, Bill would never understand women.

"Uh, I thought maybe we could change the name a bit to Hastings Interior and Architectural Designs. Hastings Designs still for short."

She sniffed in a very un-CeCe-like way. "That would be wonderful."

He still wasn't convinced. "I'm not asking for a decision now. But even if you'd rather keep our businesses separate, I'm staying." He'd been hemming and hawing, thinking about it, but as he said the words, he knew it was the right thing to do.

"I want to be here for you and Cam. I don't want to be more than a car trip away from the family. I look at the Salos, and while there might be more of them, I know that we have that family connection too. I'm not willing to give it up."

"Yes," she said.

"Yes, I'm not willing to give it up?"

"No, yes, we'll be partners. Yes, Hastings

Architectural and Interior Designs. Yes. Stay. Cam doesn't have a father —"

"He does. You just won't say who."

"Biology doesn't always count. For all intents and purposes he doesn't. But he has you. He'll have you. I couldn't ask for more for my son. So yes."

Bill hugged his cousin. "Thanks."

"No, thank *you*. But this is going to present a problem, *Carter,*" she said, using his given name to emphasize just what problem she was referring to. "I could explain to the Salos. Looking back, I realize maybe the pregnancy made me a bit . . ." She hesitated.

"Crazy?" Bill supplied.

She laughed. "Maybe. Let me explain. It might have seemed nuts, but I didn't want this job because they felt sorry for me. I don't need anyone's sympathy. I wanted the commission because my designs were the best. And that's how we got it. But there's more between you and Dora Salo than my designs, and I don't want my pride to stand in your way."

"I'm a big boy. Whatever Dori and I may or could have, I'll handle the explanations."

"Thank you, Bill. Thank you for everything."

"I'm doing it because I'm selfish. I want

to teach Cam here how to shoot hoops, take him fishing . . ." He got up. "Get some rest. We'll talk about this later."

"We will, but the answer will remain the same. Yes."

Her eyelids were already starting to droop. Bill took Cam, put him into the bassinet, then covered him up. "Get some sleep, little guy."

CeCe's eyes were already shut as he eased out of the room and closed the door.

His mom and aunt were in the hall, cups of coffee in hand.

"She's sleeping," he said.

"Good. We'll head back to the house to catch a bit of shut-eye, then come back in the morning. Are you coming?"

"I'll be there shortly."

Before he headed to CeCe's for some sleep, he wanted to talk to Dori.

He headed back to the waiting room. The rest of the Salos had either headed home or were with Vancy, but Dori was still sitting there, as he'd hoped she would be.

"I waited for you," she said.

"I was hoping you would."

"How are your cousin and the baby?" she asked.

"Great. I don't know about your niece, but CeCe's baby looks like a cross between

161

Yoda and Bruce Willis. Don't tell her I said that, though."

He'd thought she'd laugh, but instead, she offered him a tight smile and said, "I won't."

"Any chance you'd let me buy you a cup of coffee? I have a few things I want to discuss with you."

"I thought you'd never ask."

Bill's stomach was in a knot. He hoped that Dori would just laugh everything off, that she'd be happy he was staying. That's what he hoped, but to be honest, he really wasn't sure of anything other than the fact that as much as CeCe and Cam were part of his reason for staying in Erie, so was Dori.

She was a big part of it.

The biggest.

"Carter . . . or should I call you Bill?" They sat down at an empty table in the cafeteria.

She'd already heard that Carter's mother had called him Bill in front of her family, and she didn't know what to make of it.

Maybe Bill was a childhood nickname that he'd discarded as he got older. Maybe he'd even been embarrassed when his mother used it in front of other people.

Maybe.

But Dori had known Carter long enough to read his expressions, and his expression now didn't read embarrassment. It read guilt. The I've-been-caught expression she'd seen on Chris and Rick so many times.

"You heard. I figured you did, and I owe you an explanation."

"Yes, I guess you do."

"My name is Carter William Hastings the fourth. My dad goes by Carter, so I was Bill. Billy when I was young."

"But you decided to use Carter as you got older?" She wanted him to say yes. To tell her that was all it was. But there was more. She could see it.

"No. I never decided to use Carter. I've spent my life trying to be different from my father, and I never use the name we share if I can help it. CeCe, my cousin, decided for me. At the end of her pregnancy she was put on bed rest, and she didn't want your family to feel sorry for her or to think that meant she couldn't do the job, so she had me pretend to be her fellow designer to land the commission."

He'd used her. Dori let that knowledge sink in. "She let you land the commission by flirting with the head of the project for her?"

"Seriously, that's what you think?" Carter — no, Bill — looked angry.

"No, flirting with the head of the project

163

was never in Cece's job description. Pretending to be an interior designer was all she wanted me to do. She bought a bunch of outrageously expensive clothing and insisted I go by Carter. She said it was more 'metrosexual' than Bill."

"I don't understand." She didn't, but it didn't matter. She still felt betrayed. Not in a soap-opera, melodramatic way, but in a small, hurt way.

"I didn't either. Still don't. I think her pregnancy hormones caused some kind of psychosis. But she asked me, and I promised. To be honest, I didn't see the harm. I planned to leave town as soon as she and the baby were home and fine."

"You didn't see the harm in pretending to be something you weren't?"

"She's my cousin. She asked me. How could I say no?"

"And after we started to date, you kept up the ruse because you were planning to leave, so where was the harm?"

"Yes. I was honest with you about that. I was honest about everything except my name, the way I dress, and my occupation."

"That doesn't leave much to be honest about."

"Well, it gets worse, because things have changed. You see, I —"

164

"Carter. Bill. Whoever you are, it was an absurd plan. I didn't care who drew the plans or who presented them to me. I just cared that they were brilliant."

"That's what I told CeCe."

Dori wasn't quite sure how she felt about Carter's being a Bill. About his not being an interior designer at all. But she wasn't quite as angry as she'd been a couple of minutes before.

"Fine. Is that all?" Dori asked. "There are no other skeletons in your closet?"

"Well, as I said, I'm not an interior designer. I'm an architect."

"That's it?"

He nodded.

She sighed. "Okay, that's not so bad. Crazy, but not so bad."

"I'm glad you think so. But there's one more thing I have to tell you."

She felt her shoulders tighten as she prepared for the next hit. "Okay."

"I'm not leaving town."

"Pardon?"

"I've decided to stay in Erie. CeCe and I are going to form a real partnership. Hastings Interior and Architectural Designs." He paused. "And, most important, I want to keep seeing you."

"No," Dori said flatly.

"I'm sorry about the ruse, but you and I both know, if Vancy had asked you to do something crazy, you would have."

"It's not about your being a Bill. Or an architect. It's about your staying. That's not what I signed on for. I was dating you because you were leaving. If you stay and we keep dating?" She shook her head. "I'm not interested in a long-term relationship. A few more weeks was about all the shelf-life I'd planned on."

"Why?"

She didn't answer. Instead she said simply, "If you're staying, then we're done. Hastings Designs can finish the project, but we're done dating."

"I thought you understood. It wasn't that big a lie."

"Bill . . ." she began. The name felt odd at first. "Let me go through this slowly. I'm not looking for anything more than casual dates. And even those are few and far between. I like the life I've built just the way it is. I'm not interested in altering it in any way. And if you're staying, then eventually my life *would* change. And I don't want that. So, your cousin can still design the interior of the Hazard Hills house, but you and I? We're done."

"Dori, is this about Leo?"

Dori's heart sank as Bill said the name. "Who told you about Leo?"

"Doesn't matter, but is it? Because I'm not him. He left, lied, then dumped you in a horrible way. I'm staying, and a big part of that is because of you."

"If that's why, then don't. Because we're done."

She got up and walked out of the cafeteria.

She was done with Carter — Bill — Hastings.

Chapter Eight

Bill had no idea what had gone so wrong with Dori, but she held fast to her proclamation.

She wasn't going to date him.

He stopped by her house. He called. He sent flowers. He sent e-mails. Nothing worked.

If she'd stopped dating him because of his deception, he'd have understood, but breaking up with him because he wasn't moving . . . *that* he didn't get.

Cam was a week old, and Bill still hadn't made any headway with Dori, so he decided to call in the big guns. He dialed the number, knowing he'd either win an ally or be in for a tongue-lashing to end all tongue-lashings.

"Hello, Mrs. Salo? It's Carter."

"Don't you mean Bill?" Nana Vancy asked.

"She told you."

"She's my granddaughter. Of course she told me." Her voice practically bristled with agitation.

"Did she tell you why?" he asked.

"No. When I asked about you, all she said was, 'Carter's not who you think. He's not even Carter. He's Bill. And I don't want to talk about him.' So I dropped it."

"Will I be out of line if I point out that dropping it isn't something I picture as normal for you?"

He could almost hear her smile on the other end of the phone line. "It would be a impertinent comment but an accurate one. But, *Bill*" — she emphasized his name — "I've known my granddaughter longer than you have, and I recognized that look on her face. She isn't going to change her mind."

"What if I were to take you to lunch, explain my being a Bill, not a Carter, and apologize profusely? Then, if you agree it wasn't some dastardly deception, maybe you'll hear me out and help me win Dori back."

There was a long pause, and Bill thought he'd lost the battle, but finally Nana Vancy said, "A woman's got to eat, I suppose. And I've found that food always tastes better when it's flavored with a good story. And this is going to be a good story, right?"

169

"I hope you think so."

"Fine. Pick me up at noon."

Bill wasn't quite walking on air, but he felt better than he had in a week. If Dori's grandmother was on his side, he had a better chance of at least making Dori talk to him.

He hurried back to Cam's nursery. "Hey, CeCe, I'm going out this afternoon."

His cousin was sitting in the rocker, cradling Cam. "Shh!"

"Sorry." He still hadn't gotten used to having an infant around. He lowered his voice to just above a whisper. "Want me to put him in the cradle for you?"

She shook her head. "I like to just hold him sometimes. He's such a miracle."

"You're right, he is. Where's Mom and Aunt May?"

"They went to the Millcreek Mall to do some shopping for Cam. And Dad's out in the backyard, making plans for a swing set."

"Uncle John does know that Cam's not walking yet, right?"

She looked up and smiled. "Yeah, but you know Dad. He likes to be prepared."

"You're lucky."

"So are you. You might be his nephew, but he thinks of you as a son."

"You're right. I am lucky, and I am Uncle

170

John's son in every way that matters. And, speaking of lucky, I'm going out to lunch. You'll be okay?"

"I'm fine. I can't be anything else with Mom, Dad, and Aunt June here," she reassured him. "Dori?"

"No, the next best thing. Her grandmother."

"From what you've told me, she could prove a powerful ally."

"That's what I'm hoping. Wish me luck."

"You know you've got it." She felt guilty. It was written on her face. "But, Bill, I feel so responsible. I'll talk to Dori if you like."

"No. I'm going to fight this battle on my own, but thanks."

The doorbell rang.

"I'll get it." Bill opened the door to find a stranger on the porch. "Can I help you?"

The man's expression registered surprise, then anger. "I need to see CeCe."

"Whom shall I say is calling?"

"Cameron Campbell."

The name registered. "Cameron? As in the man who was dating CeCe about nine months ago?"

"You're counting?" If anything, the man looked even angrier.

"Wait here." Bill slammed the door in Cameron Campbell's face, and he had to admit, it felt rather good. He'd have liked to have slammed his fist into the man's face but had refrained.

"Who is it?" CeCe asked as he came back into the nursery.

"Cameron Campbell. I left him standing on the porch."

Her face paled. "Cameron's here?"

"He wants to talk to you."

"Oh." She sat there silently for a moment, still rocking the baby.

"Do you want me to send him away?"

The question shook her from her daze. "No. No. I'll go talk to him. Could you hold Cam?"

"Sure."

"Stay in here. No matter what, stay in here."

"Sure." He took the sleeping baby and moved closer to the doorway, ready to blatantly eavesdrop and protect his cousin if need be.

He heard CeCe open the door. "Cameron. What do you want?"

"I want you back."

"Geez, does he think it's that easy?" Bill whispered to the baby. "He walked out on your mom and you."

"Things have changed since you left," CeCe said.

"I got scared," Campbell replied. "It's not manly to admit it, but I fell for you so hard, so fast, I didn't know which way was up. So I walked. I was wrong."

"I meant it when I said things had changed. There's someone else now that you have to know about."

"He answered the door. I don't blame you, Cecilia. I didn't harbor any illusions that you were sitting here waiting for me, pining over me. And if you tell me you love him, I'll back off, but I needed you to know that I love you. That I was wrong."

Bill could hear the emotion in CeCe's voice as she said, "You've got it all wrong. The man who answered the door is Bill."

"Your cousin?"

She didn't say anything, so Bill imagined she nodded.

"So, about this other man?"

Bill realized that this man, this Cameron, wasn't quite the jerk he'd thought he was. CeCe hadn't told him about the baby. He was going to kill his cousin. A man had a right to know these things.

"Bill?" CeCe called. "Could you bring Cam out?"

As he took the few steps into the hall, she smiled. "I knew you were listening."

He shot her his best eyebrow arch to let

173

her know he'd not only heard everything but had figured out that she hadn't told Cam's father she was pregnant.

"I know," she said softly. "I was wrong."

He nodded. "You okay?"

"I am." She took the baby from him. "Cameron, I'd like you to meet Cameron William Hastings." She put the baby into Cameron's arms.

The man looked baffled. "He's mine?"

She nodded.

"I'm going to go to that lunch now," Bill interjected. "It seems you two have a lot to talk about, and now that I know you're okay . . ."

He grabbed his keys off the hall table and headed toward the door.

He could hear CeCe explaining to Cameron. "I didn't tell you because I wanted you to want me for me, not to stay out of some sense of obligation."

"I was afraid, and look what I missed. . . ."

Bill shut the door and hurried to his truck. He had a feeling CeCe was going to be all right.

Now, if only he could be sure he and Dori would be too.

He had to get Nana Vancy on his side. Then maybe *she'd* find a way to get Dori to listen to him.

■ ■ ■ ■

Dori was miserable.

It had been a week, and even working on the Hazard Hills house wasn't enough to shake her out of her funk.

It was all Car— It was all Bill's fault.

When he was Carter Hastings IV, a man who dressed to the nines, drove a girly car, and was her polar opposite, he was safe to have around. He was someone who was leaving town, someone who had a limited dating shelf life, and all that made him perfect in his unperfectness.

After his announcement that he was staying in Erie, that he wasn't quite the priss he'd been acting like . . . well, his perfectness made him absolutely a no-no. Dori had dated a perfect man once and believed that they'd get married and spend the rest of their lives together. Then he'd left her for another woman.

She was done looking for a husband.

Her promise to Nana to care more about her marriage than her wedding had been easy to make, because she never planned to marry.

Oh, it wasn't just that she'd fallen for the wrong man once upon a time. And it wasn't just that she was a Mary Ann, not a Ginger.

It really came down to statistics.

The fact that her entire family had found their perfect matches meant, statistically, her odds of finding that were slim to nil.

So why bother?

She'd decided that a long time ago, so why was Bill Hastings still on her mind?

Her cell phone rang, shaking her from her funk.

"Hello?"

"Dora Lee Salo, I expect you at my house tonight for dinner."

Her grandmother's voice said there was no arguing, but Dori didn't want to see anyone, so she tried. "I don't think I can, but —"

"Don't *but* me, and don't give me excuses. I am your grandmother, and you're coming to dinner. Be here by five."

Her grandmother hung up.

Dori stared at her cell phone for a full minute before flipping it closed.

Great. Dinner with her big, happy, everyone-in-love family.

That's just what she needed.

Bill was nervous.

"You're sure?" he asked Dori's grandmother. "You're sure she'll come?"

"You have met me, right?" she asked with a laugh. "My grandchildren all know better than to stand their grandmother up."

"Fine."

"Now, Bela, he's going to take me out for a long, romantic dinner — right, Bela?"

Dori's grandfather was shooting Bill eye-daggers. "I still think we should stay and keep an eye on this one."

"Bela Salo." That was all she said as she stood, tapping one foot.

Looking at Dori's grandparents, a person would assume that Bela, so much bigger and stronger, led the family. But even Bela Salo, clan patriarch, listened to the tiny dynamo who had been his wife for decades.

"Yes, *szívem,* I'm taking you to dinner. Then we'll come home and check on this one."

"Sir, I want to apologize again. Really, I am going to be a partner with my cousin. It was mainly just a name and clothing change. She thought it was important, and she . . . she was pregnant." There. Bill wasn't proud. But he'd played the baby card, and he watched as Dori's grandfather's expression changed and softened.

"Yeah, there's that. I've dealt with pregnant ladies, and I know about humoring them."

"Thank you, sir."

"Tell you what, *Bill*. If my granddaughter forgives you, I might see my way clear to forgiving you as well. But you'll have to do your best to make and keep her happy."

"That's my plan, sir."

"Fine. Vancy, my love, let's go to dinner."

"There's the chicken paprikash we made in the kitchen, and dobos torta in the fridge. Feed her, woo her, Bill. And when the time comes, let me plan the wedding."

"I'll do my best."

She crooked a finger, beckoning Bill to lean down. When he did, she kissed his cheek. "See that you do. And call me Nana Vancy. Everyone does."

With that, she took her husband's arm and led him out of the house. All that was left was waiting for Dori.

Waiting and thinking.

Dori was in a fine mood by the time she pulled up in front of her grandmother's.

No other family members' cars were in the drive.

As a matter of fact, even Papa Bela's car was missing.

Why on earth had she been ordered to put in a command performance while everyone else remained free? Where was the fairness in that?

Her grandmother was going to have a fit that she'd shown up in work clothes, but she'd been tied up with the electricians on the site and was lucky to have made it at all.

She threw open the front door and was hit by the smell of chicken paprikash.

She'd know the smell anywhere. It was one of her favorite dishes.

"Okay, since you made my favorite, Nana Vancy, I've decided to forgive your curtness on the phone," she called as she walked back into the kitchen.

"Hello, Dori."

"Car— Bill. What are you doing here?"

"You wouldn't see me. Wouldn't answer my calls. And desperate men resort to desperate measures. I enlisted your grandmother's help."

She shook her head. "I can't believe she'd help you."

"I took her to lunch and told her everything. She agreed that you're being unreasonable."

"I'm not."

"Do you want to sit down and have dinner? Your grandmother said it was your favorite. She let me help make it."

"You've been with her all day?" Dori

asked, sitting on one of the counter stools.

"Since lunch. Your grandparents left for their own dinner a bit ago, and I finally had time to think. I've got some things to say to you."

"Fine. Say them, and when you're done, you'll leave me alone?"

"Yes. If that's what you want."

"Fine." She nodded to the stool across the counter from her. "Talk."

Bill took the seat. "I was going to apologize again. But while I waited for you, I finally caught my breath and analyzed everything that's happened. The past week I've been so intent on chasing you that I hadn't really done that."

"So you were analyzing. Good for you. Okay. Now we're done?"

He shook his head. "I was analyzing, and I realized that it's not that you're mad that I'm a Bill, not a Carter. To be honest, you'll be more comfortable with Bill."

"Maybe, but you still lied."

"CeCe and I are forming a real partnership. I want to call it Hastings Interior and Architectural Designs. She wants Hastings Architectural and Interior Designs."

"Leave it Hastings Designs, and add 'Architectural and Interior' as a subtitle."

He nodded. "That might work."

180

"Great. We've solved your professional crisis. Are we done?"

"No. My point is, it's not that I pretended to be an interior designer either. It's other things that are upsetting you."

"So, Freud, hit me with your best analysis."

He cocked his head and studied her a moment.

She couldn't help but feel uncomfortable. "Stop that," she said.

"It's not that I'm Bill or that I'm an architect who wears regular clothes, not that designer stuff. It's that you still think you're Mary Ann."

"I told you as much."

"Leo convinced you that you were right."

"Leo?" She tried to look nonchalant but wasn't sure if she managed it. "He's barely a blip in my memory."

"*And* you think it's a matter of statistics."

She faltered. That was the crux of it, but she wasn't sure how Bill had so accurately echoed her own thoughts.

He kept going. "I was fine to date as long as our relationship came with an expiration date. It was safe. But I'm staying, and I still want to see you. That scares you, because you don't believe, statistically, that you can find what the rest of your family has."

She wanted to ask how he knew, how he could read her like that. But she tried to act as if his insight didn't bother her. "Okay. So maybe that's a part of it."

"All of it together makes you believe we can never work out." He crossed his arms over his chest and looked smug in his ability to sum her up.

"There you go. You've figured it out. But it doesn't change the fact that I don't want to date you." She started to stand, but he reached across the counter and took her hand.

"But you're wrong, Dora Lee Salo. I'm not a statistic. And I love you. That trumps all odds."

"Are you done?"

"No. Because I know that all of it — your Mary Ann-ness, Leo, the idea that if everyone else in your family's found a soul mate, you can't — they're all excuses. Because you're afraid."

"I'm not afraid." She laughed, trying for scoffing but afraid it had fallen flat.

Bill still held her hand. "My cousin told me her baby's father was out of the picture. I assumed he'd left because he didn't want the baby. But the truth was, she was afraid to tell him, afraid he'd stay with her out of

182

a sense of obligation, not because he loved her."

"I can understand that. I wouldn't want someone to stay because he felt he had to."

"I agree. But he deserved to be told. He came back, came back for her, and found out he had a son. Because she was afraid, he missed her pregnancy, missed Cam's birth."

"I'm sorry."

"And you, you're just as afraid as CeCe was. You're afraid I'll leave like Leo did. You're afraid you won't find what the rest of your family's found. Dora Lee Salo, you're afraid."

"Stop saying that."

"Then prove I'm wrong."

"How?"

"Date me. Agree to see me. Agree that there's something between us and we should explore it."

"Look at me." She gestured at her work clothes. "This is as good as it gets. Dusty work clothes and weird hours. I'll never be a traditional girlfriend."

"Who wants traditional? For instance, when I ask you to marry me, and you say yes, I'm completely prepared to let your grandmother plan our wedding."

"What?" *Marriage?* He was talking about

183

marriage?

"I know it's fast," Bill continued. "I just thought I should put it out there."

"I haven't even agreed to date you yet."

He was grinning now. "But you will. I know you wear work clothes. So do I. We both like sunsets and fishing. I like your family, and I suspect, after dealing with your own, that my family won't intimidate you at all. But more than liking that you're a Mary Ann, not a Ginger, I love you for it."

"What?" Dori was pretty sure she was losing her mind. Or maybe Bill was. Either way, there was some major sanity impairment going on.

"Dora Lee Salo, I, Bill Hastings, love you."

"You're crazy."

"Not quite the response I wanted, but I'll wait." He paused and added, "And I have one more surefire reason I know you'll agree to date me."

"What?"

"I learned how to make chicken paprikash. Your grandmother assured me that that, in and of itself, would make me completely irresistible to you."

She laughed then. Laughed because all of a sudden her fears seemed absurd. Laughed because for the first time in her life, she was glad she was a Mary Ann. Laughed because she was looking at a man she . . . she loved.

Even though part of her ached to say the words, she didn't. "I'm not saying I love you too — I think it's too soon."

He didn't seem overly concerned. "I'll wait."

"But I will say . . . I think I could love you."

"We could shake on it, but I have a better idea."

"What would that be?"

He pulled her into his arms and showed her.

Later, as they ate dinner, Bill said, "I think we should have a short engagement."

"I haven't even said I loved you."

"And as for our wedding, while I was thinking earlier, I thought about your family curse."

"Wow, you really were doing a lot of thinking."

"Yeah, I worked a lot of things out. Including your grandmother's curse."

He told her what he'd figured out, and when Dori stopped laughing, she said, "You know, Bill, you're going to be a handy man to have around. So, what are we going to do about this?"

He told her his plan.

CHAPTER NINE

"What is all this?" Nana Vancy demanded.

Despite her week-long depression, she still managed to infuse her words with a regal certainty that her question would be answered.

No one said anything as they looked at Dori expectantly.

"Go on, sis, you figured it out," Noah prompted. Vancy nodded in agreement.

"Nana, it's a party for you!" Dori yelled, "Now, boys!" Chris and Ricky pulled the strings, and the cover over the banner dropped. "See?"

Nana Vancy turned and read the banner. "Salo-Family-Wedding-Curse-Ends Bash? No," she said sadly to Dori. "You and Bill eloped. The curse hasn't ended."

"Nana Vancy, Bill figured it out. You've had it wrong all along. The curse ended years ago when you and Papa Bela married. There never was a curse on the family, just some very unlucky wedding mishaps."

Nana shook her head. "It's sweet of you to say, but I know what I know."

"I know you don't like to hear it, but you're wrong. You've been wrong from the beginning. Every member of our family cared more about their marriages than the wedding. You and Papa didn't wait to plan another wedding. After he finally arrived, all you wanted was to be married to him, to start your lives together. The minute you said your vows, the curse ended. After that, it was more of a blessing than a curse."

"But . . ." Nana Vancy tried to wrap her mind around the idea and finally shook her head. "No, it couldn't be that simple."

"Vancy was ready to marry the wrong guy. And look what happened. She found Matt."

She looked at Vancy, holding little Stella, wrapped in Matt's arms, Ricky and Chris at their sides. Her sister nodded. "It's true, Nana. I'm happy."

"And Noah and Callie? Why, even Julianna has found her true love in Darren." Callie and Julianna, stepsisters and friends, nodded, as they moved closer to their husbands.

"And me, Nana," Dori said. "I thought I was humoring you when I swore I'd break the curse for you, because I never thought I'd find my true love and need a wedding.

And I guarantee you that I didn't expect the man I'd fall for to come wrapped in a metrosexual, designer-suit-wearing package, but there you are. I've gotten my happily-ever-after as well. Don't you see? There is no Salo Family Wedding Curse. There's just a Salo family legacy of true and everlasting love."

"And your Bill figured this all out?" She eyed Dori and Bill, who looked so right together. So happy. So in love.

"My Bill is a very smart man." Dori leaned closer to her husband and waited before she repeated, "Nana, there is no curse."

Vancy Bashalde Salo started to cry. Cry in earnest. Bela put a giant arm around her and held her tightly. "There, there. It's all right. The curse is over. It never even really got started."

"I know. That's why I'm crying."

All these years, all these worries. And there had never been a curse?

She looked around the party at her family and knew in her heart that Bill and Dori were right. There was no curse, just a legacy of love.

Later, much later, as the party wound down, Chris and Rick came over to Nana Vancy, and Chris said, "Tell us a story, please."

"About your wedding to Papa Bela."

Nana Vancy patted the couch, and the boys sat down, one on either side of her. "When I was young, in Erdely, Hungary, I was the mayor's daughter, and many of the men my age wanted to marry me, for I was beautiful. My hair was as black as yours and your Aunt Vancy's, and my eyes were very blue. Yes, many men wanted me, but there was only one I wanted."

Ricky supplied, "Papa Bela."

She nodded. "I only had eyes for Bela Salo. I was lucky, back then, and Bela fell in love with me too. He wanted to marry me. My father encouraged me to plan the biggest wedding the town had ever seen. I was sure everything would be perfect."

"But Papa Bela didn't show up," Chris said.

"Right, my Bela wasn't there. I thought he had abandoned me. I was heartbroken and angry —"

Chris nodded. "So you said the words."

"I hope Bela never gets a big, beautiful wedding like this."

"And you said you hoped no one in his family ever had a big, beautiful wedding, 'cause it would make you remember that you didn't get yours," Chris prompted when she got lost in the past and stopped the story.

"Right," she continued. "I said the words because I was hurt and couldn't stand the thought of watching my Bela, and someday his children, have the wedding I didn't get. But in my pain, I forgot that words have powers."

"And when you remembered, you were sorry, and you went into the woods and said . . ." Ricky waited.

"I said I wanted to undo that curse. But if I couldn't take back the words cursing Bela and his family to unhappy weddings, then let me add that it wasn't my intention to curse Bela or his family to a life without marriage or love. Just no big weddings that meant more than the marriage itself. I'm afraid that's what happened to me. I thought more about the wedding than what came after. So when the day comes that someone in his family cares more about love and their marriage and less about their wedding, then please, please let that break my curse."

"Then Papa Bela came back," Ricky said. "He'd been in an accident."

"I was so happy to see him, so happy to know he really did love me, I never thought about waiting for another big wedding. No, that very day we found a minister and got married, just the two of us and our families. I didn't think anything else about those words I'd said until my own children all missed out on their big, beautiful weddings for one reason or another."

Chris knew the whole story by heart and supplied the next lines. "And then you wanted Aunt Vancy, Uncle Noah, or Aunt Dori to break the curse for you."

She nodded. "I did."

"But you were wrong," Ricky said.

"Yes, this story doesn't end the way I thought it did. It seems there is no family curse. There's just a big family so filled with love that every marriage is a blessing."

John Warsaw, the reporter who'd made Vancy's life a living hell after her fiancé left her at the altar, piped up from one side of the couch. "Mrs. Salo, may I quote you?"

She looked at the reporter and smiled. "Yes, you may."

Family Curses Turns out To Be a Blessing
by John Warsaw

Vancy Balshalde, the beautiful daughter of the town's mayor, lived in Erdely, Hungary, and planned a big wedding to Bela Salo. . . .

191

Maybe it just goes to show, the things you think are curses can turn out to be your biggest blessings. Rather than cursing her family to disastrous weddings, Vancy Bashalde Salo bequeathed her family a legacy of love.

ABOUT THE AUTHOR

Award-winning author **Holly Jacobs** has written over twenty books. She's a lifelong resident of Erie, Pennsylvania, and is happily married with four children. She credits her family for everything she knows about love and laughter. You can visit Holly at www.HollyJacobs.com or mail her at PO Box 11102, Erie, PA 16514-1102.